A pleasant assortment of short stories that makes you smile and gives you hope.

~ Independent Book Review

An Anthology Edited by
SARA-MEG SEESE

PIVOT

Stories of Change

Featuring Award-Winning Authors
KELLEY RENE, BOB RICH, AND PAULA PECKHAM

Palm Branch
PUBLISHING

Congratulations to the authors who contributed to this anthology. It takes courage to put your thoughts and imaginings on paper for all to read. We appreciate the trust you put in us to launch your work into the world.

Table of Contents

Beginner's Luck 15

The Perfect Cup of Masala Tea 31

Vishnu Weeps 43

The First Girl I (N)ever Kissed 59

To Walk In The Park 73

The Greatest Gift 101

The Olde Tobacco Bullion Shoppe 115

Artist's Revenge 135

Teaching Young Kids 147

The Brother 159

November or Never 177

Rising Sublime 195

Renewal 211

A Crazy Little Thing Called Love. 225

About the Editor

Sara-Meg Seese is a graduate of Ursinus College, where she built her love for reading into a B.A. in English Literature. After graduation, she toured for more than fifteen years with an international Christian repertory theater company, racking up thousands of performances in English, German, and Spanish. The New Jersey native finally stopped traveling and put down roots in the DFW area in 2005. A pastor's kid twice over, she has written and produced a number of plays and skits for local churches and had a monologue published in a nationally-distributed magazine. Several short stories and novellas have been featured in various anthologies, including Amazon best-sellers, and she was thrilled to receive a Reader's Choice award in 2018. Her day job as a Software Quality Analyst allows her to get paid to break the computer system on a daily basis, a challenge she relishes most of the time. She shares her little condo with four feline overlords who enrich her life while depleting her bank account with their addiction to salmon pâté and handfuls of treats.

Introduction

WE LIVE IN a world full of choices, more so than at any other time in history.

Think about it. Two hundred years ago, young men and women rarely chose the person they'd marry. One hundred years ago, the local movie theater showed one movie each week, and everyone shopped at the neighborhood grocery store. Fifty years ago, there were three main television networks. Ten years ago, office workers wouldn't imagine working from home, much less the freedom of a hybrid schedule.

We can choose to eat out, cook at home, or use Doordash. We get to decide if we'll have Asian, Italian, Tex-Mex, or good old American hamburgers and fries. Want a caffeine break? Coffee comes hot, frozen, or cold-brewed, with soy milk or almond milk or nonfat whip, drizzled with chocolate or salted caramel, supercharged with extra espresso, or blended with hazelnut or lavender.

Want to watch a movie? There's a multiplex at every mall and two hundred channels on cable. For the cord-cutters, there's a plethora of streaming subscriptions. Roku and Firestick offer 24-hour broadcasts dedicated to true crime aficionados, language learners, DIYers, or wannabe chefs.

But even with so many options available, most of us end up doing the same-old-same-old.

The Roku algorithm always recommends the cozy mysteries and character-driven procedurals to me . . . but just in case, I've got two channels "favorited" at the top of the screen. No sense scrolling down three dozen times when I'm just gonna watch another rerun of SVU!

If I go to a restaurant, I scrutinize the entire menu—but I still end up ordering the franchise's version of a Chicken Caesar Salad. If I'm feeling rambunctious, I might opt for Chicken Alfredo with Broccoli. No way will I venture to have that North Carolina Pulled Pork or the Coconut Curry Pad Thai.

Let's face it. Humans don't deal well when faced with too many choices. Twelve-Step programs insist that people will only break their bad habits if staying where they are becomes more painful than embracing the positive changes they're offered. We opt for predictability over passion and fight to maintain the status quo instead of indulging in random acts of spontaneity. A wide variety of options is more likely to lead to analysis paralysis than the exhilaration of freedom.

Even major life events are usually a matter of inexorability rather than opportunity. When I got married, I didn't really make a decision—I simply took small, obvious steps along the relationship highway. I went on a date with a friend, then a second date, and then more dates. When we were apart, we wrote letters and called each other on the phone. We talked about getting engaged, we shopped for rings, we set a date (and changed it twice, for family and convenience). Sure, he popped the question on bended knee, but he already knew the answer I'd give. On the Big Day, I woke up, had my hair and makeup done, put on a pretty dress, said the words, and went to the reception . . . but nothing changed other than my last name. Decades later, my marriage ended without even a whimper, the inevitable result of a slow slide into apathy and failure. A lawyer and I stood in front of a judge for ninety seconds, I answered two questions, and the divorce was final. Not only was it uncontested, my ex didn't even show up.

But this anthology showcases another, more adventurous way to navigate the journey through life.

Because the human experience is not simply an implacable series of checkpoints along a predestined path. As ephemeral as the wind, as intangible as beams of light peeking through the clouds, between one breath and the next, liminal moments arise. A small change can alter one's entire trajectory. These critical junctures might seem small, but they become sublimely meaningful with 20/20 hindsight.

The characters you are about to meet will be faced with opportunities to do the unexpected, to try something new, to adjust their worldview or step out of their daily routine. They've been given fictional life by an international group of authors with authentically diverse voices who dared to put pen to paper and write something *different*.

These protagonists range from a boy on the cusp of manhood fumbling through an awkward first date to an elderly woman making peace with the ghosts and gods of her ancestors. Acquaintances become partners, and casual encounters become enduring connections. Their relationships are woven of threads as fragile as tea leaves and as powerful as maternal love, tested by betrayal and restored by faith.

Don't get me wrong. They don't have it easy. None of us do.

Dynamic change only grows in the soil of relinquishment. It's rooted in resolution and watered by resilience. It is nourished by creativity and blossoms in the sunshine of optimism. It requires the willingness to look beyond superficial appearances and the fortitude to endure challenging circumstances.

Sometimes long-term plans conflict with an amazing, unexpected alternative. Other times, fulfilling—or resurrecting—a lifelong dream necessitates venturing beyond comfort zones such as financial stability or even hearth and home.

Without courage, there can be no change.

In the last analysis, then, the stories in this anthology are about courage. When faced with the metaphorical fork in the road, these fictional people head for the road less traveled. They choose the variation, not the theme. And the outcome is better than they could have ever imagined. At the pivotal moment, they decide to rise. Their lives . . . and their world . . . will never be the same.

Those of us at Palm Branch Publishing hope that you find inspiration from these stories.

Taste that exotic menu item at a restaurant you've never been to before. Click on a new station and watch a show in a genre that breaks all the algorithms. Introduce yourself to a stranger in the checkout line or invite an acquaintance to a home-cooked meal. Dust off your resume and apply for that career change. Take up a new hobby. Rediscover the magic of a childhood dream.

Go for it!

Embrace the adventures ahead. Weigh the alternatives. Gather your courage. Explore your creativity.

Pivot. Start by turning the page.

Maybe . . . just maybe . . . your life will never be the same.

BEGINNER'S LUCK

By Sylvester Chikelue Nnoli

Waabri desires one thing above all else: wealth. His pursuit of it starts in school then meanders through manipulation, deception, and incarceration. In the end, he learns wealth comes in many forms, and he had what he desired all along.

Sylvester Chikelue Nnoli is a prolific writer and dedicated advocate for marginalized voices. Born in Jos, Plateau State, Nigeria, his academic background in the study of religion enriches his diverse literary pursuits. He's been featured on platforms such as Mooncafe, People's Poetry, NoiseMedium, and Nircle, among others, and specializes in crafting articles that boost businesses' Google search rankings, bridging the gap between effective communication and digital visibility.

Nnoli's storytelling earned him accolades in the January 2016 Storried short story contest and the January 2024 African Unveiled contest, launched by *Nircle*. As a member of the Association of Nigerian Authors and an active participant in the prestigious Mindportal Penstar Club, Sylvester Nnoli remains committed to using his voice to inspire change. For more about his work and insights, connect with him on LinkedIn.

Beginner's Luck

Sweat beaded on Waabri's forehead in Mogadishu's noonday heat. He bent down and whispered into the ear of his niece, Calaso. "Just because something is possible doesn't mean it is probable."

Thousands of people had gathered for the grand finale of this year's Image Creation Prize. Their long wait for the announcement of the winner was about to be over, and they fixed their gazes on the Master of Ceremonies. They cheered wildly as he celebrated the contestants.

Intent on the speech, Calaso waved a wobbly arm to shush her uncle. A flash of nervousness tightened her face, as if she had a premonition.

Waabri wiped sweat off his forehead. Every time he'd predicted he'd lose the grand prize, Calaso had encouraged him to have faith. Now, when he needed a cheerleader the most, she was silent!

"There's great creativity among the shortlisted contestants," she had said when they arrived. "But yours is creative, too."

Settling himself firmly in his seat, Waabri did his best to hide his doubts about the quality of his submission. He looked around the great hall, which was teeming with people. It seemed like the whole city of Mogadishu waited, abuzz with anticipation over the annual prize.

Above them, a beautiful blue sky offered no protection against the sun that beamed high above the festivities. On the dais, the Master of Ceremonies described the history of the contest in detail while the crowd applauded his eloquence with every sentence.

His fingers itched to draw the scene. At least that would help fill the time until the speech would finally be over.

Waabri's thoughts wandered back to a boy of fourteen with an over-embellishing imagination and not a bit of interest in history.

Young Waabri's pencil scratched and etched its way across the page, forming shoulders, brows, and lips. Yes, soft, delicate lips.

"Everyone stand on your feet." His high school teacher's instructions barely registered in the drone of the lecture.

Waabri concentrated on the finishing touches on his picture. They would not take long. A flip here and a flip there. *Perfect.*

"Waabri!"

His pencil seemed to know exactly when to dig in for a deep edge or tilt ever so slightly for a faded shadow. The face on the page took on dimension, and he felt a rush of joy.

"Waabri! What are you doing?"

Startled, he tried to get up, but his feet tangled and he fell off his seat.

The room erupted in laughter.

"I will suspend you from my class! Bring that nonsense you are doing over here immediately." The teacher's sharp words doused his creativity like water on a rock.

Waabri slowly carried the piece of paper to her while his classmates snickered.

She took one glance. Her eyebrows rose and her eyes widened, brightening like the sun rising over the horizon at dawn.

"Did you just do this? I'm flabbergasted." She didn't move for several seconds while she stared at the drawing.

Finally she sighed. "Quiet, please. You all know better."

The students stopped talking and formed a line.

"Waabri, you have great potential. But you cannot do this during class." She meted out his punishment with clemency, but she kept his drawing rather than tearing it up.

At the end of class she handed it back to him. "Hold onto education, as it is the key to every endeavor." She smiled. "I've never seen an eagle fly with broken wings."

From that moment, Waabri had a pencil in his hand and a sketchbook in front of him constantly. Every single event in Waabri's early life pointed in the same direction. He *knew* he was born to create images. He even imagined himself winning the annual prize, basking in the admiration of the whole city of Mogadishu.

When his father died, leaving him the oldest child and only son, he had to take care of his mother and his three sisters. He sought wealth—the get-rich-quick kind of wealth. He put down his sketchpad and found a job.

He sighed, remembering, and dabbed at the beads of sweat on his forehead.

The Master of Ceremonies was on a roll, shouting into the microphone like a Sunday morning preacher. "But in life, one cannot dispute the fact that there are certain things you can't leave behind no matter how you try. And when one is patient, opportunity will always present itself."

Waabri clapped in agreement.

His niece gave him a startled look.

He reached over and squeezed her shoulder. He was proud of her, of their whole family. She had been sheltered, growing up, but it hadn't turned her sour like so many other young people. She never took her good fortune for granted.

Unlike her childhood, growing up in Mogadishu had not been a bed of roses for young Waabri. He had usually felt a tinge of frustration, even after he left school. He pictured his life as a book, and each new day meant a new page to write his story. At the turn of each page, he experienced the good, the bad, and the ugly side of life.

With a résumé in hand that shone like the stars, he applied for an office job in a reputable firm in the heart of Mogadishu. He stood tall in the midst of the rest of his family when an invitation for an interview landed at his doorstep. What a big relief at last!

"I know it's time, I must make it," he told his mother, embers of hope glowing in his heart. He barely slept the night before the interview, wondering what they might ask. But of course, it didn't matter, because he would perform as confidently as he would on a theater stage.

He left at dawn, black suit freshly pressed and shoes well-polished. He excelled at the interview and received an offer of employment after a couple of days. His joy knew no bounds. He spread the good news to everyone who cared to listen.

On his first day, Waabri knocked confidently on the door marked Human Resources.

"Come on in." A huge, dark woman in her late thirties gestured for him to take a seat. "I'm Bishaaro."

She had been one of the people who'd interviewed him, but Waabri sensed a change in the woman's demeanor. A document hung from her outstretched hand. "This is your appointment letter, but you can only earn it with a price." She leaned toward him and fluttered her lashes in an outrageous show of attraction.

Waabri flushed as he accepted the letter. She couldn't know that Waabri's heart belonged only to Axlami, his longtime girlfriend. He turned, ready to flee.

The huge woman grabbed his arm. "I see something intangible in you. Think about it. Give me a call." She slid a card into his pocket.

Sadness overcame his first-day-at-work joy. Waabri found himself in a dilemma. He needed the job, but he didn't want to cheat on Axlami. His discomfort increased each time he tried to find a solution. He dreamed about seeing a corruption-free Somalia someday, somehow. But impropriety infected small firms as well as federal levels.

Axlami noticed a few days later. "What is eating you up so much?"

He couldn't answer her, but an idea struck him. He decided to call Bishaaro and set an appointment to meet her in a guest house located in the outskirts of Baidoa.

Bishaaro welcomed Waabri warmly as he arrived. He played along with her open display of blind lust, but when Bishaaro went to the rest room to freshen up, he quickly positioned a video recording device to capture their encounter.

She came out of the bathroom, wrapped in a towel, and went straight to him.

He held her at arm's length, in the perfect position where the camera could pick up every word. "I'm really glad I have the job. But I'm curious. What would have been the outcome if I had rejected your offer?"

She raised her eyebrows and smiled. "Then you would have started to look for another job."

"Surely not." He teased her, stroking her cheek with a finger. "Do you mean you would've used your position as hiring agent to manipulate me into an affair?"

"You're here." She grasped the towel with her fingertips as if to entice him toward her. "It worked, didn't it?"

The towel dropped, but he turned away and moved out of her reach.

His phone rang. Waabri fumbled to answer it. "Oh, no! My uncle? He died? I'm on my way and I'll be there soon."

Taking two long strides for the door, Waabri snatched the recording device and tucked it into a front pocket.

"Waabri!" Bishaaro shouted. "Where are you going?"

He didn't bother with a farewell, leaving Bishaaro alone in Baidoa.

The scene went viral the next day.

Bishaaro lost her job, and Waabri grew anxious. As much as he wanted to correct the insanity going on in his society, he knew one evil often begets another. He stayed alert, determined to shield himself from any revenge Bishaaro might pursue.

Months went by without any incident. Waabri believed great endings came from small beginnings, and he began to relax, feeling liberated, accomplished in his mission of making his country less corrupt.

So he was surprised, that January day, when Bishaaro's attempt at retaliation caught up with him. He'd washed his favorite shirt and left it spread outside to dry. Just as he picked it up and turned to go back indoors, he glimpsed movement along the fence. He took cover behind a large flowerpot, scarcely daring to breathe as two masked gunmen broke through the front door of his house.

Waabri took to his heels. He couldn't go back home. He knew the men wouldn't stop searching for him until he was found.

Waabri scampered through the shadows, weaving in and out of the bushes until he reached the home of his childhood friend, Rooble.

Hiding in the shade on the side of Rooble's house, Waabri peered through the partly open window.

Rooble lounged on the sofa, just inside. His cell bobbed in the air with every movement while he laughed and blew kisses into the phone. "We should run off together. Just you and me."

Just as Waabri raised a hand to tap the pane, he saw Axlami's face on the screen.

"You know I'm engaged to Waabri." Axlami smiled at Rooble, her teasing expression clearly framed by the video call.

"But you love me."

"I do, but he has a much better job."

Waabri's heart skipped a beat as his fiancé and best friend playfully flirted back and forth. How could they do this to him? Axlami had embraced him with open arms. Rooble was like a brother.

He sank to his knees.

He couldn't go back to his house, where the gunmen waited. He didn't dare go back to his job, for surely they would watch there, too. Rooble had betrayed him. And his worst fear—losing Axlami—had come true.

Once again, Waabri was out on the street.

He clenched his fists and got to his feet. *I have seen worse things in life. This will not break me. Trying times make a man tough.*

Insubstantial as the wind, he roamed the streets, inhaling the cold air and sleeping under bridges. The sky wept with him, pelting him with heavy rain drops.

Hungry and shivering, he sought shelter at a local night club in the neighborhood, but the bouncers denied him entrance. He held his ground, begging for assistance.

One of the bouncers grabbed him at the nape of his neck, pulled him close, then shoved him toward the street. Waabri retaliated, pushing back against the bouncers.

A brawl ensued.

Waabri channeled his grief and anger. He towered over the six foot three bouncers. They took turns trying to subdue him. He battled them like a physically fit, well-trained fighter. When the dust cleared, Waabri stood, breathing hard, while the other three lay on the ground, too dazed to get up.

"We need to talk." A stocky, pot-bellied fellow introduced himself. "I'm Dan, the night club owner. You lookin' for work?"

That street fight earned Waabri employment at the night club as a bouncer.

Within seven months he was bored, discouraged by low wages. He couldn't make a great living this way.

"Let me tell you about Endeavour. They're always looking for new cage fighters who have what it takes." Scott, one of the club's regulars, approached him one night. He was a huge guy—about Waabri's size—but light skinned. He had an extravagant nature that had earned him admiration. "You're a natural. And you can earn a lot more than you do here."

Old habits die hard! With a few training tips from Scott, Waabri fought with vigor and stamina. Nicknamed "Blow," he racked up wins that translated into big payouts. He basked in the throaty roar of those who cheered him on. Night after night, fight upon fight, Blow became an undefeated fighting sensation. His fame grew, and his spirits soared like an eagle all the way to the bank.

Gamblers bet large sums on him and even sponsored him to go abroad to fight. The stars aligned in his favor, and he remained undefeated.

Until that day in Utah, when he was matched against The Great Terminator, a stone-faced, bearded gladiator from Mexico.

Even now, sitting in the great hall back in his home city of Mogadishu, he could remember every swing, every punch, and every dirty trick. It was the worst fight of Waabri's life, the one that almost cost him his life.

The Great Terminator had a reputation for underhanded strategies. That night, he threw a fistful of sand into Waabri's eyes. A slimy move, no doubt, but in a cage fight, there were no rules. The Great Terminator pounded Waabri with continual attacks, while evading Waabri's blind counterpunches easily. Soon Waabri fell to one knee, off balance, weak, and staggering under the blows.

The Great Terminator reached for Waabri's neck and twisted it, sealing his victory.

But Waabri lay on the ground, unable to move.

An ambulance rushed him to the hospital where for an entire year he would convalesce, learning to walk again, while medical bills ravaged his life savings.

With constant pain, hawking drugs on the streets seemed the only way he could earn money again. Despite the battle his conscience waged against him every time he dropped a wad of bills into a mailbox, this high was too sweet to resist.

But it came at a cost. He was apprehended during a police raid and sentenced to six years in prison.

His fist tightened in fury even now at the memory. All those wasted years felt like slavery all over again.

But Waabri could see now how his time in jail—day after day, month after month—was not truly wasted. While he was incarcerated, his memories and experiences began to take shape. He wanted a do-over, a restart in life. This was the time he needed, the protection he needed, to make a new plan for himself. He vowed he would not waste his life again. His heart of a lion saw him through, in this place where only the strong survived.

One day at lunch, bored as usual, Waabri took one of the napkins and sketched a prison guard with a face like a rock.

His fellow inmates were amazed.

The guy sitting on his right nudged him. "I wouldn't believe you did this if I hadn't watched the whole thing."

Another picked up the napkin and tilted it, examining it carefully. "I sure would like a portrait to send to my girlfriend. But it has to be good, y'know?"

Waabri shrugged. "I've got paper in my cell."

"A pack of cigs says you can't draw my mug." One of the tough guys scowled at him, arms folded in challenge.

"Deal," said Waabri.

He earned those cigarettes by dinner time. Soon all the guys were asking for images of themselves.

Could drawing be his fresh start? He knew there probably wasn't much money in it. Maybe not even enough to pay the bills once he got out. But what if it was possible?

He started sketching every chance he could get. He didn't have much to fill his days, and he found he enjoyed honing his craft.

One afternoon, the warden paused at his cell door. "Waabri."

Waabri stiffened, and he slowly rose to stand at attention. The man was tough enough to have been a former cage fighter himself. The inmates stayed out of his way whenever they could.

"I have a favor to ask."

Waabri's heart pounded against his ribs as he waited to hear more. What might a favor from the warden entail?

The man stepped closer and leaned in before speaking. "I've seen your work. It's very good."

Waabri inclined his head respectfully, cautious but curious. "Thank you."

"I'd like you to draw my portrait. One that captures my persona—" He hesitated, as if trying to conjure the right words. "I want a portrait that shows my strength and dignity. As warden of this fine institution."

Only one form of payment would prompt Waabri to honor this request. "And in return?"

Waabri knew of the warden's reputation and didn't want to get on his bad side, but he also knew an opportunity like this had potential.

"I can offer you clemency." The warden narrowed his eyes. "But you'll be deported back to Somalia."

Home! It had been so long since he had seen his family, his city.

He bit his lip. "How do I know you'll follow through once the portrait is done?"

"My part is already done." The warden pulled a folded paper from an inside pocket of his uniform and handed it to Waabri. "You just need to do yours."

Sitting here now, baking in the summer sun, Waabri smirked. That was one of the easiest jobs he'd ever done. And what a celebration his friends and family enjoyed with his return to Mogadishu. It was as if nothing had changed. And yet, everything had changed.

He stretched his arms to the sky, relishing his freedom.

Calaso reached for his hand. Her admiration for him was evident. She'd been the first of his entire family to encourage him in his craft. She'd cheered loudest when he'd agreed to enter the contest. She'd been the one to celebrate with him when his submission was shortlisted for the grand finale. He had so much to thank her for.

"Can you feel my heartbeats?" Calaso whispered. "I can no longer control them."

"It's normal, niece." He stretched his right arm and gripped her shoulders. "Everything changes in a man, except the beat of his heart."

Calaso leaned her head on him in a momentary stillness, fixing her gaze on the stage.

Waabri tensed, knowing the lucky one soon would be crystal clear. All of the shortlisted contestants were very good.

He'd created a superb image, but how it would compare to the other entries was yet to be revealed. Each of the shortlisted contestants were already known and well established in the craft. Some had already earned past awards. Only Waabri was considered a beginner among them.

A man in a white suit casually made his way upon the stage. A paper in his hand flapped at his side, mocking all who anxiously awaited the results. He observed every protocol in his speech, acknowledging the dignitaries who made this year's prize an immense success. Pausing, he glanced down at the paper.

The entire hall hushed.

"The winner of the third prize is..."

Waabri held his breath. But his name wasn't called.

The audience erupted in applause as a young woman two rows ahead plowed her way to the center aisle, then went onstage to receive her trophy.

Dropping his face to his palms, Waabri tried to find his equilibrium. The excitement was too much for him.

"The winner of the second prize is…"

Waabri didn't look up. His stomach turned and churned, tempting him to flee the assembly, but the clapping, yelling crowd penned him in place.

"And the moment we've all been waiting for…"

Waabri tucked his head in between his knees to drown out the chaos.

"Uncle! Uncle?" Calaso tugged his elbow.

Waabri tilted his face just enough to see past the shelter of his forearms.

Jumping in place and laughing, Calaso pointed at the stage. "You won! You won!"

A shockwave started in the pit of Waabri's stomach, edged up his esophagus, and dried up his throat. Dazed, he strode to the stage.

"One more round of applause for this year's overall champion, Waabri!" The announcer greeted him with a vigorous handshake, then presented the grand prize—a huge trophy and a check for one hundred thousand dollars.

Who says beginners don't have luck?

THE PERFECT CUP OF MASALA TEA

By Sunayna Pal

The art of making the perfect cup of tea requires patience and attention to detail. In this realistic fictional piece, cultural expectations, relationships, and personal habits add to the delicate mix.

Sunayna Pal's poetry graces the pages of numerous international journals, anthologies, museums, poetry festivals, textbooks, and libraries, resonating with readers worldwide.

Her debut book, *Refugees in Their Own Country* (B&W Fountain), vividly narrates the Partition of India through evocative verse and illustrations, while her second book, *Please Go to the Park* (Bottlecap Press), is an invitation to embark on a journey of self-discovery. As the Director of The Poetry Academy, Sunayna nurtures a deep appreciation for poetry in others. She is dedicated to Heartfulness meditation.

Residing in Maryland with her family, Sunayna invites readers to explore her work and journey at *sunaynapal.com*.

The Perfect Cup of Masala Tea

I LEANED BACK in my cozy swivel chair, ready to head into the kitchen to start making lunch, but the soft hum of the room was interrupted by my husband's purposeful stride. He marched toward me, trusty blue cup in hand, his scrunched-up nose a sure sign of what was to come. Instinctively, my fingers found their way to the sides of my head as I braced for the impending conversation.

He held the cup before my face. "Can you remind me how to make tea?"

With a feigned air of nonchalance, I turned my chair to face the computer screen, pretending to be engrossed in work. "Not again. We just discussed this last week."

He looked at the cup, wrinkling his nose. "Please! This doesn't taste or smell perfect like yours." He held it in front of me again. "What am I missing? You know about the project deadline and the stress—"

I pushed the cup away. "There is nothing I do to make the tea special."

"It must be something. Is it the measuremen—"

"I eyeball everything." I interjected, my tone bordering on curt.

"Do you have a specific order? Or a ritual like the . . ."

"Like the Japanese tea ceremony?" I threw my hands up and turned toward him. "Please! Come on now. It is everyday Indian masala milk chai."

He took a sip. "No, this isn't. I don't even know what this is. I follow your recipe and end up with this. Taste it."

"I don't feel like drinking tea at 11 in the morning. Thank you. I have to—"

He gasped. "What kind of Indian are you to refuse tea?"

I took a deep breath. "Enough. I know what you will say. It is impo—"

"Yes! In Indian culture, it is impolite to ask your guest if they would like to drink tea—without actually making it and offering it to them. And here you go, refusing—"

"What do you—"

"Please share the recipe one last time?" He smiled.

"No. Please. I am drained." I shook my phone in front of him. "Besides, Mom and I just had an argument."

He scoffed. "Did you tell her to cut down on drinking tea?"

I crossed my arms, but before I could say anything, he kissed me on the shoulder. "Please tell me the recipe for the last time. I won't bother you about tea after this. Promise."

I took a long breath. "Measure some milk in your cup and transfer to a saucepan. Add a pinch of tea leaves and some grated ginger directly in the milk and let it all boil once. Then simmer till you smell the desired fragrance. Strain. Add sugar and enjoy."

His eyes narrowed—he still didn't believe me.

Before he could comment again, I said, "I promise you I don't do anything else. Now you keep your promise."

And . . .

he did . . .

for that day.

It has been over six months since that promise, and he has broken it several times. With each passing day, the weight of his work projects seems to multiply, each deadline blending into the next. Still, he hasn't given up attempting to make that perfect cup of tea, although he continues to fail.

In his defense, he doesn't try every day because I fear that he would be addicted like my mom, who drinks tea like she is drinking water. When she worked in the Indian Excise department, she had a fresh cup of tea every two hours or so. I can imagine the workers of the canteen, making and serving tea, washing utensils, and brewing more, from the start of the day till the end. After retiring, my mom still drinks at least four cups every day. There is a family joke that my mom's blood group is T+.

I didn't realize the depths of my husband's despair until I overheard him talk over the phone. "She's hiding her secret— there must be something. Did she learn it from you? What's your ritual?"

I guessed it was my mom. He was silent as she detailed her method. But then, his glowing face became dejected, like a drained teabag. He saw me, averted his eyes, and gulped.

I felt sorry for him. "Do you want me to make tea in front of you?"

"Why didn't I think of it before? I have a work call in twenty minutes."

"As always," I murmured.

"Twenty minutes is enough to make tea?"

"Um—"

"Okay, after the call. I've waited for so long . . . Also, I have to revise something before the meeting."

The work call went on for hours, and he forgot about the tea.

The next morning, as I rolled my yoga mat away, he walked toward me with a smile on his lips. "Dear?"

"Let's make tea."

He followed me to the kitchen with a tentative eagerness, his demeanor akin to that of an excited child on the verge of discovery. As he settled into a chair at the kitchen table, I could sense the anticipation radiating from him, a palpable energy.

With a practiced hand, I reached for the saucepan. Its surface gleamed dully in the soft light filtering through the window. With a quick rinse under the cool stream of water, I placed it on the stove.

Turning to the fridge, I retrieved the familiar milk bottle. My hand steady, I filled his beloved blue cup to the brim.

With a fluid motion, I emptied the contents of the cup into the waiting saucepan, the milk cascading in a steady stream as it mingled with the metal below.

I switched on the stove, and his smile widened.

As I added half a spoon of tea leaves, he asked, "Aren't you having your own heavenly tea?"

I shook my head.

"I have never understood why. Your mom drinks a lot of tea. Didn't your dad drink tea too?"

"Yes, he had it twice a day."

"Then how is that you don't drink?"

He continued to watch me with fascinated attention. I held his gaze for a few seconds, and he raised his eyebrows in question.

"My dad had predicted that I would drink two cups a day like he did when I would start a monotonous corporate job. He has had his regular two cups of tea since he was twenty—the same age he started working. Even after he retired, he continued to drink two cups. One after breakfast and one after his nap. Maybe I didn't find my workspace boring. Enough to say that his predictions didn't come true for me."

He looked at me as if he wanted to know more. This is how he would look at me during the first weeks of marriage.

"You know this already. I enjoy tea sometimes, but don't feel the need to drink it every day. I like to think of it as medicine. If I feel a cold coming or if I didn't sleep well, I make myself a cup of ginger tea. Besides, I don't like something having control over me."

His eyes didn't leave me as I spoke. It reminded me of the days when we were first married again. He used to spend so much time with me. Doing things, I liked or just hang around me to be with me or listen to me talk about me.

I held his gaze.

He didn't question me.

I felt like staying in that moment forever.

I turned toward the fridge to remove a piece of ginger, quickly peeled away the skin with a paring knife, and cut it into small flakes.

As if he understood my thoughts, he walked up and hugged me from behind. "I know I have been busy with this project lately. Things will be better soon, I promise."

Two years into our marriage, I knew how important his career was for him. I sighed, hoping things would improve. I knew he was present when he was needed, but any free minute had him jumping back to work. His work took priority over me and starting a family.

The milk sizzled as it came to a boil and our attention diverted to the tea again. I reduced it to a gentle simmer as I turned to him, catching his gaze fixed intently on the pan.

I joked "A watched pot never boils."

"What?"

I just giggled.

He gestured at the tea. "Anyway, it is simmering now. It won't boil."

"It will if you give it enough time," I reminded him softly as I removed a few leftover Parathas out of the fridge for breakfast.

He bent over the saucepan and took a deep breath. "I can smell the tea."

"Of course you can if you smell it that way. Let it simmer."

"I've always wanted to ask you why you use a saucepan."

"As opposed to a kettle?"

He nodded.

"Because water evaporates from the milk in the saucepan and makes the tea creamier."

He leaned close and looked at me. He'd washed his hair with the coconut shampoo I loved.

His phone chimed. "Shucks, I have a meeting."

I took a deep breath and smiled. "Go on. I'll bring the tea to you." Then I readied his cup with a strainer.

"How will I learn?"

Ignoring his question, I applied ghee on the Paratha and let it warm on the cast iron griddle.

"We have a microwave that works." He pointed, a teasing smile on his face.

"I like the Paratha a little crispy. Do you want one?"

"No. Tea is enough for me. What's next? Will you stir? All the tea powder and leaves are attached to the cream."

"Yes."

"How many times?"

My fingers went to my head again.

"Okay, you don't have to answer that," he said quickly, "but how much longer will you keep it like this? I can smell the tea."

"I am letting it brew."

He darted out of the kitchen. I watched him go and couldn't help but sigh at the whole situation. He might never learn.

But he quickly returned with his cellphone and headphones. Adjusting himself on the kitchen stool, he smiled. "I will learn how to multitask."

"Yeah, right."

He ignored my comment and joined his meeting. I lifted my perfect brown Paratha with tongs and slipped it onto the plate. He checked into the meeting, and I heard him say his greetings.

The tea ballooned up like a cupcake, which he should have observed. This was also the time for the robust aroma to fill the house. I stirred it once and tapped the spoon on the saucepan, but he was occupied with his call.

So much for multitasking.

I strained the tea into his cup. Stirring the sugar with a spoon, I walked toward the kitchen table.

I quietly placed his cup near him. He glanced up, and I tried not to grin as I walked to the porch to enjoy my breakfast.

I heard him take a slurp of the smooth liquid and let out a satisfied "Aaah!"

I couldn't help but giggle again. We didn't cross paths for the rest of the day. So much for spending more time with me. I knew he wouldn't change. If only he could spend a little more time . . .

The next day, when I finished tending the plants on the balcony, I stepped back into the living room and found the familiar smell of tea in the house. Then I saw him, sitting proudly by the window with a tray and the biggest grin I had ever seen.

I walked to him and found two cups of tea and a few Khari biscuits.

"Let's sit and chat like old times." He nodded. "I've got your secret."

VISHNU WEEPS

By Michaele Jordan

Na Tao lives in fear of the mysterious footsteps in the night. When she enters her father's special room to examine his compelling sculptures, her father mistakes her interest as a love for art. After years of admiring his collection from afar, she must address his questionable dealings and her greatest responsibility.

Michaele Jordan was born in LA, educated in New York, and lives in Cincinnati. She's worked at a kennel, a Hebrew School, and AT&T. She's a bit odd. Now she writes, supervised by a long-suffering husband and two domineering cats.

Her first novel, *Blade Light*, was serialized in Jim Baen's Universe, followed by her period occult thriller, *Mirror Maze*. Her stories have appeared in Buzzy Mag, Fantasy, and Science Fiction, Abyss and Apex, and Perihelion. Horror fans will enjoy her 'Blossom' series in The Crimson Pact anthologies. (We're trying to negotiate a chapbook.)

Her website—michaelejordan.com—is undergoing reconstruction, but just grab your hard hat and come on in.

Vishnu Weeps

THE NIGHT WAS warm, but the little girl pulled her blanket around her ears and turned over in the narrow bed until she was completely cocooned. "I'm not afraid," she whispered to herself. "There's nothing to be afraid of."

They could not pass through a locked door. She had secured it herself, heard the *click* that proved the fastener had engaged. Even if they could get into her room, none were large enough to hurt her. Even if they wanted to. And why should they? Their room was bigger, after all. They were probably very happy there. They'd never tried to get in before.

Even if they did, they were just a bunch of big dolls.

Nothing to be afraid of.

Still, their footsteps in the next room, soft, steady, and unending, did not sound like they were happy. More like the cats at the zoo, pacing back and forth along the cage walls, searching relentlessly for a way out.

But the cats never found a way out of their cages, and neither did the walkers in the next room. The little girl fell asleep, still reassuring herself that she had nothing to be afraid of.

Next thing she knew, it was morning.

She always got up early, before Nanny could bustle in and help her dress, which usually meant Nanny picked something ugly for her to wear. Nanny would counter any protests, insisting her father *particularly* liked to see her in the nasty outfit in question, even though he'd never said so. Much better to choose her clothes and dress herself.

She opened the door and peeked out. Downstairs, Cook and Nanny argued about something, their voices shrill but their words jumbled. Just like they did every morning. Which gave her a chance to dart over to the next room without being seen.

Papa's office, lit by the morning light, sucked her in instantly.

She walked past every pedestal, her daily ritual, to verify that *they* were all where they were supposed to be.

None of them had moved.

The sad lady was still half-turned to look behind her, one hand raised to her mouth. The dancer balanced on the toes of one foot, with her other leg raised and her palms pressed together in prayer. The wise old man sat cross-legged, his head slightly bowed. She tiptoed through the room, intent on her task.

"Na Tao!"

She whirled.

Nanny stood at the door with her scolding face on.

Na Tao bit her lip.

Turning around to face a tall man, Nanny curtsied. "I am so sorry, Dr. Jacoby. I've told her and told her she is not allowed in here, but she slips past every time my back is turned. I'm at my wit's end. Perhaps we should lock the door?"

"I didn't touch anything, Papa!" Na Tao squeezed her hands together. "Really, I didn't, I promise! I only looked!"

Papa chuckled. "Are you already an art lover, little peach?" He turned to Nanny. "Perhaps we should sign her up for art lessons, Nurse Delory."

Nanny bobbed her head. "What a wonderful idea, sir!" She leaned forward. "Na Tao, would you like to take art lessons?

We could get you some modeling clay and you could learn to make your own sculptures. Would you like that?"

Na Tao was pretty sure that Papa was joking. She'd already had drawing lessons, and they hadn't gone well. "Not really, ma'am. If you don't mind."

Papa laughed. "So you'd rather just look at sculptures instead of making them yourself? Either that's the grossest laziness I ever saw or an amazing philosophically enlightened detachment."

"Not just any sculptures." Na Tao hoped she wouldn't be asked to explain what philosophically enlightened detachment meant. "Your sculptures are special."

"Do you think so?" For once, Papa didn't sound like he was laughing at her. He sounded interested. "Maybe you really are a budding art lover. Come here."

He took her hand, and her fingers curled around his warm palm.

Nanny shrugged and left them with an aggrieved sigh.

Papa led her inside the office. "Which is your favorite?"

She darted to the low bookcase beside the desk and pointed to the statue on top of it. "This one!"

A stone man with the head of a pig knelt on one knee, holding one arm around a tiny lady who stood on his raised leg. The lady smiled up at him, and Na Tao felt he was probably smiling back—although it was hard to be sure, because of his tusks. His head was not like most pigs—it was lean and graceful. Elegant.

Na Tao waved at the tiny lady. But the stone figure didn't wave back.

"Really?" Papa patted her shoulder. "I'm impressed. You have uncommonly sophisticated taste. That's Vishnu as

Varaha, and it may be the best piece in my collection. It's nearly a thousand years old."

She caught her breath. No wonder she wasn't allowed to play in the office! "The book I got at the museum says he's rescuing the earth goddess from a terrible demon."

"Well, aren't you clever!" He sat in his chair and drew her into her lap. "So, if you know so much, do you know who that is?" He waved toward the corner of the desk.

"It's the Buddha. Or at least it's supposed to be." She giggled. "It looks like a girl to me."

He laughed with her. "It does to me, too. I've always wondered if it were mislabeled. Maybe it's really some Jayavarman queen. But I didn't mean the statue. I meant the photograph."

In the picture next to the Buddha head, three men posed formally in front of a podium and a flag. An unfamiliar man stood on one side of her Papa. She picked up the framed photo and pointed at the other. "That's the man who came to dinner last week."

A very special occasion! Wearing her party dress, she'd followed Nanny downstairs to be presented to the guests. It had been a small gathering, but all done up with candles, crystal goblets, and a lace tablecloth.

"Yes, my dear, he certainly did. Do you remember his name?"

She hung her head and shook it slightly.

"His name is Lon Nol, and he's the president of Cambodia." Papa's lips twisted. "At least for now."

Na Tao gasped. "The President? No wonder we got out the lace tablecloth. He actually came to dinner at *our* house!"

"And came a long way to get here, too—almost five hundred miles. He's hoping I'll get him some money." Papa pointed at the other man in the picture. "That's their Prime Minister, Norodom Sihanouk. I got him some money once, back during the civil war when he was king. I thought he'd keep quiet about it—he was so desperate and ashamed." Papa shook his head sadly. "But apparently he told Nol all about it."

Nothing in that sentence that made any sense at all. Didn't civil wars usually end with getting rid of the king? Unless he won. But if he won, wouldn't he still be king instead of Prime Minister?

She gave up and set the framed picture in its spot next to the Buddha head.

"Do we really have that much money?"

"Not exactly. But I know how to get it. I just need somebody important to give me permission to sell the statues."

She looked around the room. Nanny said Papa's statues were valuable.

"Sell the—not the Vishnu, please!" She jumped down from his lap and backed away, as if she'd suddenly found herself snuggling with a stranger.

"Oh, absolutely not!" Papa patted his leg. "I would never sell my own statues. I love them too much. But there are plenty more to go around—enough for everybody. In fact . . ." He lowered his head as if to whisper a secret into her ear. "If this deal goes through, we may be getting some more soon. Would you like that?"

"More? Like these?"

"Not exactly, but similar." He smiled at her. "Would you like to help me choose? What kind do you like best?"

She bit her lip. "I don't exactly like most of them . . ."

"Then why are you always sneaking in?"

"I want to make sure they're still here. You'd be so upset if they left."

"Left?" He shook his head. "You think maybe somebody would steal them?"

"No, nothing like that. But I worry they'll run away."

"Sweetheart . . ." He leaned forward and pulled her back into his arms. "You don't have to worry about that. They're just statues. They can't move by themselves."

"Yes, they can," she whispered. "They walk at night."

He stared at her. Obviously he thought she was making it up.

"They do! I know they do! I can hear them padding around." She rubbed her eyes so she wouldn't see the disbelief in Papa's. "Maybe they're not trying to get away. Maybe they're just visiting with each other. But they do. They walk at night."

Fifty years later, six thousand miles away in her adopted country, Na Tao got the phone call she had been dreading for years—ever since the ugly rumors about Papa first surfaced.

"He's not doing well. He wants to see you." The unfamiliar voice on the other end of the line brooked no nonsense.

She went immediately to the expensive mansion he'd bought when he'd left Cambodia for the last time. Her hand shook as she rang the bell. "I'm looking for my father. How is he?"

The housekeeper who opened the door, tall, thin, and very British, let out an aggrieved sigh so much like Nanny's that the years almost vanished. "The doctor is here. He's having more tests done."

Naturally the housekeeper let her in anyway and made her a cup of tea. "They take his blood so often I'm surprised he has any left."

"He's all right, isn't he? My Papa?"

"You'll have to ask his nurse about that." The woman shrugged. "Make yourself at home. I'll take your luggage upstairs and get your things sorted for you while you wait."

Na Tao carried the fragrant brew as she wandered the house, visiting the statues. Some she'd never seen before, but most were old friends.

Her heart cried out when she saw them, clustered in her father's modern mansion with its thick carpets and rectangular rooms. They looked incongruous, out of place, lost. Had they heard the rumors, too?

Silly, of course. They were statues. They couldn't answer. What did words like *trafficking* or *looted artifact* mean to a piece of sandstone? Did statues care where they were or how they got there? Or how much money had changed hands in the process?

"Papa told me once that he was doing you all a favor." Hands on her hips, she glowered at the pig-man's accusing snout and the tiny woman's slumping shoulders. "Finding good homes for the others. Not leaving you to be bombed into rock-dust."

She knelt by her father's desk and let her gaze connect with the Buddha head. "He gave you—he gave them—a safe haven from the war."

But was that really what he had done?

Did they miss the ancient temples, after all? Or was this terrible accusation made against her father the reason for the sorrow she had always sensed in them?

She lifted the Vishnu down from the bookcase to the floor. Sitting cross-legged, she wrapped her arms around it and nestled her chin between its ears. She whispered to it, words in a language she hadn't spoken aloud since childhood.

Papa found her there, in his office, after the doctor finished his house call. "You didn't need to come all this way just to see me. I'm fine."

He didn't look fine. He looked . . . old. Tired. Sad.

She hugged him. He returned her embrace, but his arms held her loosely and his body seemed light and fragile as a bird's.

Letting him go, she turned away and set the statue back into its place on the bookshelf. "Did you ever notice, there's a little streak in the stone, just under Vishnu's eye?"

"I did." He coughed, a soft sound like clearing his throat. "Several people looked at it, but they all agreed it's just an impurity in the sandstone. There's no harm, and nothing can be done about it anyway."

She nodded. "I thought as much. And I kind of like it. It almost looks like a teardrop. Makes him more human, don't you think?

He smiled. "You always had a soft spot for the Vishnu."

Na Tao followed him to his bedroom. "I didn't get a chance to speak to your doctor. Is there anything I should know?"

"I don't want you worrying and fussing over me. It's mostly old age. I'm pushing ninety."

"But what does he say?"

Settling into bed, he patted the spot next to him. "Come. Sit next to me."

She pulled over a chair instead, since she planned to stay with him for more than a few minutes. But she was close enough to cup his hands inside hers, letting the warmth from her body radiate into his cool skin.

"The doctor says it's my heart. I found out they're going to file charges against me." He closed his eyes. "I'm innocent, you know. I didn't steal anything. I made proper arrangements with the proper people."

"Of course you did." She pushed conviction into her voice, although she was far from certain herself.

"It was a war. The money—the money . . ." He turned his head away, breathing hard. "The men came from the government. They brought the statues to me. Trucks . . . trucks full of crates. The money was for the war."

His side had lost. Meanwhile, she'd attended the best schools, accompanied her father to innumerable festivals and awards events wearing a never-ending supply of designer evening gowns, and learned, much to her embarrassment, that her classmates and co-workers considered her insanely wealthy. She'd spent her life surrounded by priceless Asian art, had become an expert herself, although she never felt comfortable buying or selling pieces with cultural or spiritual significance.

What would happen to her Papa if he was charged with—what, exactly? Or by whom? He was not a thief. All the statues had been given to him. He'd kept them safe.

Hadn't he?

She lifted his hands to her lips, pressed a gentle kiss. "I love you, Papa."

Her vigil lasted two nights and two days. The doctor visited each morning, but he didn't do much other than listen to her father's chest and make notes on his chart. The housekeeper kept her supplied with tea.

She'd just drifted off to sleep, leaning onto the side of the bed, her cheek cradled against his hand, when he stirred.

"Do you hear that?"

She held her breath, straining her ears. "What, Papa? What do you hear?"

"Footsteps."

Her skin prickled.

"They're walking." He took a ragged breath. "Back and forth. Back and forth."

"Who, Papa?"

"*They* are. Can't you hear them?" He tugged the sheet until it covered his ears. "Lock the door so they can't get in."

"Papa, there's no one there. Just you and me." But she knew better. Even as a child, she'd known.

He whimpered. "And them. They walk at night. You know they do. You've heard them, too."

"They're statues. They can't move. They can't hurt you, so there's nothing to be afraid of."

Nothing to be afraid of.

She told herself that, over and over, while his breathing rattled in his chest, while she waited for the next inhalation, and the next, and the next, until the next one didn't come.

Letting go his hand was the hardest thing she'd ever done.

She went downstairs, into his office, and called the doctor. She touched the tiny dancer, the cross-legged old man, the Buddha that looked like a girl. Gently, she took the Vishnu from its spot on the bookcase and placed it in the center of her Papa's desk.

Only then did she let herself cry.

More than a year later, she finally returned to the country where she had been born.

King Norodom Sihamoni himself arranged to meet with her. "The Minister of Antiquities has told me about your one-woman crusade. '"Cambodia's gods and treasures must come home."'

She smiled at him. "You look just like your father."

"You knew Norodom Sihanouk?" His eyebrows arched in surprise.

"No." She shook her head. "I did not have that honor. But my father did. He often spoke of him." She took the old photograph out of her purse, caressing the frame before she showed it to the king. "This was always on my Papa's desk. There's my father, with President Lon Nol and, of course, yours."

"Father was Prime Minister at that time, I believe. Judging from the clothes and style." His lips quirked. "Times have changed."

"He would talk to me about you, too." She met the king's gaze, hoping he could read her sincere conviction. "Papa believed it was a miracle that your father's name, your father's son, and your father's ideals endured through so much heartbreak and tragedy to emerge triumphantly as the guiding light of this beautiful nation."

The King gallantly kissed her hand, as cosmopolitan and suave as if he were truly French and not just raised there while his father was in exile. "You have a way with words, Na Tao."

So she said it one more time. "Cambodia's gods and treasures must come home."

Arrangements went swiftly after that. Most of her father's treasures would be housed in the National Museum of

Cambodia, at least until construction of a new museum was complete.

But it seemed only fitting that her father's lovely Buddhas should reside in a Buddhist temple. The Silver Pagoda lay within the grounds of the Royal Palace, near the remains of King Norodom Sihanouk, under the protection of the Emerald Buddha. The Silver Pagoda wasn't limited to Buddhists—it welcomed all the King's subjects and sheltered many alternate gods and historical relics.

So Na Tao hand-carried the last case to the installation ceremony. It held one final gift for her people, a gift that was not a Buddha. She unlatched the fasteners, opened it, and lifted out her beloved Vishnu.

"You were getting pretty heavy," she whispered to the statue.

She placed the Vishnu on the pedestal that had been prepared for it and rubbed her aching arm. Now that the moment had come, it seemed terribly hard to say goodbye.

"Dear Vishnu, I have done my best." Folding her hands, she bowed to the figurine. "Won't you please stop walking now? You're home at last. Surely you can rest."

She stroked the stone cheek gently, just under his eye, one final caress. Her finger came away damp, as if a tiny teardrop had fallen there.

THE FIRST GIRL I (N)EVER KISSED

By Jerry T Watkins

Adolescence, friendship, and budding romance are themes in this coming of age story set in small town America in the summer of 1964, where a single memory of Sandra still lingers in the air.

Jerry T Watkins was born and raised in the south in the 50's and 60's.

He loves telling stories but loves writing them even more.

After dropping out of high school, Jerry went back to school as an adult. He was inspired to write by Ms. Jay Bartels at Gulf Coast Community College. He jokes that she must've worn out a dozen red pens correcting his essays. He's very thankful she stayed after him because his final essay that year won an award.

He's a married, retired, father, grandfather, and born-again Christian.

The First Girl I (N)ever Kissed

LONG HOT SUMMERS spent in Stewart, Alabama were the best of times and the worst of times. (I've always wanted to say that in a story.)

My first date was a bit of both.

I'm not sure what made me think of this particular emotional trauma this morning, but almost as soon as my eyes opened, recollection invaded my brain like a hangover. An old song on the radio might have triggered it, or perhaps the drippy, sweet smell of honeysuckles on the warm breeze. Whatever it was, this long-forgotten memory came up, and I was immediately transported, an unwilling participant, back in time.

First, I retraced the years. So many years. Great years. We're talking several wives and kids and grandkids ago. But there were gaps in the story I relived. The brain is amazing at storing memories . . . even when it brings memories up without request. They just seem to be there. After a while, the really painful memories stop coming to the surface, because the brain protects us by hiding them, keeping them away from recall.

Most of the memories and experiences during the summers spent in Alabama are incredible and wonderful, warm and fuzzy. Like Grandma and Grandpa, and porch swings, and homemade ice cream. Shelling peas and frying fish.

The memory that came up this morning was not like those.

I recalled the events of a particular embarrassing Saturday somewhere around the summer of 1964. For me, telling a story from memory usually means I had a very random memory or two, and in order to fill in the gaps I embellish it with things that may or may not have actually happened. (Such is the case here.)

My brother Robert, my cousin Phillip, and I were inseparable during those long hot barefoot summers in Hale County, Alabama. Lazy days at the creek—fishing or swimming or anything else we could think of. In the country, kids get to roam around from one adventure to another—for the most part—without adult supervision or interference. Imagine if you will, these three young Watkins boys let loose on the unsuspecting small town of Stewart. No red lights, no stop signs . . . just a post office, a flowing well and a country store.

I was the tall one, blond, with a tan from the long days spent in the sun.

My brother Robert, the quiet one, was two years, a month, and twelve days older than me—but who's counting?

Phillip was the Obi-Wan Kenobi of all things Alabama. He taught us how to catch a snake without getting bitten and where the plum tree with the sweetest fruit known to man grew. He showed us how to snatch a musk melon from Grandpa's garden without getting caught. From him, we learned that when we heard the train horn in the distance, we had just enough time to run to the crossing and watch the mechanical arm snatch the bag of mail. It moved so fast you could not see the mailbag leave. If you blinked, it just vanished, like Obi-Wan Kenobi disappearing right in front of Darth Vader's eyes.

My brother and I were considered city slickers because we lived in Lynn Haven, Florida, and knew very little about fishing, catching snakes or crawdads, or even what-in-the-heck is a muskydine. (I realize the correct spelling is muscadine, but I spell it the way Obi-Wan Phillip pronounced it.) Phillip fully embraced his role of teacher and accepted the daunting task of showing us how to be a kid in Stewart, Alabama.

It seems like we were always throwing something, aiming at anything, and making a game of it. We spent hours down at the railroad track chucking rocks at the glass insulators on the phone poles while waiting for the train to flatten the pennies we put on the rails. We lobbed rocks at the bull in the pasture, tossed acorns at each other, and on and on. We only had one bicycle between us, so when boredom overtook us we took turns pedaling downhill from Mr. Duncan's house as fast as we could, while the other two would throw green acorns as the rider passed by. The rules were you had to take your shirt off, and you couldn't pull your hat over your face. Those little things, thrown with enough velocity, would actually leave a welt. (What can I say, not everything we did made sense or made us look very smart. But we had fun!)

These were impressionable years, and during those summer days a lot of different things made an impression on me. Two of these were Tone and her younger sister Sandra. I learned in later years her name was actually Taun, but we pronounced it just like our teacher, Obi-Wan Phillip, did . . . Tone! These two girls lived in a very nice house on the left as you headed down White Road toward Big Lake. (A third thing we were taken with was their cousin Amy Jewel, who lived a little further down where the black top road stopped. But beautiful Amy Jewel will be a whole other story right by herself.)

To three young, highly impressionable, hormonal, and ignorant adolescent boys, this stretch of black top was the path to female perfection. Looking back on those days, we were quite taken with these three Bama beauties, but they were *not* impressed with us. We would make up excuses to wander down this stretch of road, hoping to catch a glimpse of any of them—excuses like "Lets walk down to Big Lake and go fishing," or "It's a good day to visit Amy Jewel's brother Paul Henry," or "Let's go throw rocks at that bull in the pasture." Sometimes we couldn't think of a good reason, but we would just haul off and walk past their houses for the heck of it. We hardly ever saw them, but that didn't stop us from endless bouts of teenage humor and boy-talk about what might happen if we did.

Being the youngest, I was the least experienced and most ignorant in the fine art of wooing a woman. Like young boys, my knowledge of girls had been acquired from watching TV, listening to older friends and my brother, and—of course—the occasional magazine. In other words . . . I had been misled and lied to! This lack of accurate, factual, truthful information would set the stage for the events of the Saturday night in this story. I now know this was by far the shyest and most awkward summer of my life. (My wife laughs when she hears me say I was very shy growing up, but a lot has changed since then.)

The first girl I never kissed, who lived in the house on the left, was a little older than me. "Older," to an adolescent boy, meant she was *much* wiser and *much more* experienced. Girls mature more quickly than boys, and at this stage of life my maturing had not even gotten started yet. (Sometimes my wife tells me mine has yet to start.) If the lovely Sandra, the object of my affection, were telling this story, she might title it, "The Summer That Watkins Boy Didn't Kiss Me." It's all about perspective.

Phillip's older and wiser brother Richard had a date with Tone, the older sister.

Richard was the hometown football hero and had quite the reputation as a ladies man. He had a slow southern drawl and a special way of smiling while tilting his head slightly to the right. You pretty much knew, when you saw that smile there was going to be something worth listening to. He would start telling a story and would soon have you totally hooked, eagerly hanging on every word. Then, when he couldn't hold it in any longer, he would burst into laughter—and you would know you had been totally had.

Tone was breathtaking, sweet, and friendly . . . and way out of our league. She was the epitome of the cheerleader, homecoming queen, valedictorian persona. Not to mention she was probably three or four years older than us three ladies-man wannabes. That didn't stop us from wishing and hoping, but in reality, she wouldn't give us the time of day.

As the big date approached, her parents told Tone she would be responsible for watching her younger sister that night. Sandra, of course, began teasing Tone about how her hot date with Richard Watkins was *not* going to happen. Richard and Tone were not happy in any way, shape, form or fashion. (I don't know what that phrase actually means, but my mother used to say it all the time.) Their ingenious plan to enable them to still go on their date required Sandra to pick one of us three Watkins boys to accompany her. Like on a date.

I said to myself, "*Are they serious? Did I hear that right?*"

Yes, it was true . . . and music to my young, inexperienced ears. One of us was about to be in the back seat with Sandra for an extended amount of unsupervised time, riding around Hale County, Alabama.

Sandra would not choose between us, so we decided to go odd-man-out to see which of us would win the dating prize. In case you're one of those rare people in the world that do not know what odd-man-out is, I will break it down for you. If three people flip a coin and there are two heads and one tail, the tail wins the contest.

Robert, the oldest, flipped our only coin—the last remaining penny that the train had not flattened—and it landed on heads. Obi-Wan Phillip then tossed the penny in the air and expectantly watched it all the way to the ground, only to see it also land on heads. Robert laughed and Phillip groaned loudly. If mine landed on tails, I would win the right to accompany the girl of my most recent Alabama dreams on my very first date.

I trembled as I tried to hold the coin steady in my sweaty hands. In my haste, I accidentally dropped it without flipping it.

It landed on tails.

Robert and Phillip began hollering in unison, "No-no-no-no-*nooooo!*" and wouldn't let me count it as a valid toss. So I had to go again. What would I do if it didn't land on tails? What the heck would I do if it *did!*

I breathed in and my trembling, sweaty fingers launched the coin skyward. All three of us watched in sheer agony as it flipped over and over. It landed in the loose gravel driveway. None of us breathed as it landed on edge, and just as in any good story, it began to roll. It traveled about three inches and finally fell over, tail side up.

With that fateful coin toss, I won the chance of my short lifetime to spend an evening with tall, cute, skinny-legged, dark-haired Sandra.

When I finally took a breath, I sounded like the guy that had been held underwater for five minutes and was finally permitted to inhale. I sucked in air with that dramatic, deep, loud gasp, like I was breathing for my very life.

My young mind was instantly flooded with one question . . . "What in the hell was I going to do now?"

About sundown Richard pulled in the driveway of Grandma's house and picked up the most immature, inexperienced, freshly scrubbed boy in all of Hale County. If my friends back in Lynn Haven could have seen me, they would not have believed it. But honestly, you just can't make this stuff up. (Well maybe you can, but that is not the case here.) I was absolutely scared to death!

In the hours since that fateful coin toss, I had been subjected to every crude, inappropriate, crass, sexist joke that teenage boys could muster up. Y'all can't imagine the stuff the older Robert and Obi-Wan Phillip told me. Needless to say, I was confused and conflicted. In hindsight, I realize they were messing with me, and I don't think they knew any more than I did.

As we were pulling away from Grandma's house, I turned and looked through the rear window and mustered up the biggest "I'm going to see Sandra and you're not" grin possible. In answer, my family—my best friends, my compadres—each flipped me off with both hands as high in the air as they could reach.

During the five-minute ride to the aforementioned stretch of asphalt, Richard kept looking in the rear-view mirror at me, laughing. He finally asked, "Have you ever even kissed a girl?"

"Are you crazy. Of course I have. Many times!"

He could tell I was lying, but really didn't care. I was just a speed bump on the way to his date with the amazing Tone.

I remember like it was yesterday . . . Sandra's light-colored dress came just above her knees. Her dark hair was fixed and pulled back on the left side with a pearl barrette. White sandals hugged her summer-tanned feet.

I opened the car door.

Just before she got in, she leaned over and whispered, "I would have picked you."

My heart was already beating fast, but her soft words made it feel like it would explode at any moment. I could smell her rose-scented perfume. This was surely the closest to heaven I had ever been or would ever be.

Time stood still. I have no idea how long we drove around listening to music on the AM radio. I remember "Hang On Sloopy" came on, and the three of them talked about how good the song was. I had never heard it before, but on this night, sitting in the back seat next to Sandra, it instantly became my favorite.

Suddenly we stopped. I didn't know where we were or how we got there but I didn't care! Richard turned the ignition off and sat there for a few uncomfortable minutes. He whispered something to Tone, and they got out and walked somewhere into the darkness of the Alabama night.

Sandra and I, alone at last, sat silently in the back seat, somewhere in Alabama, with romantic music playing on the radio and a chorus of crickets serenading loudly.

I have never been more terrified in my life.

She took my right arm, pulled it around her, and rested my hand on her own right shoulder. I was sure she could hear my heart pounding and feel my palms sweating. She was more beautiful than I had imagined. She looked up at me with those dreamy brown eyes.

Beyond nervous, I began talking—or more likely babbling—ninety miles an hour, trying in vain to ease the awkward tenseness of the moment. The darkness, the music, the situation—heck, even the crickets—seemed to be screaming out for me to kiss the girl. Looking back, I know she wanted me to kiss her, even expected me to kiss her ... but sadly, I didn't know how.

Everything I had learned about girls up to this point seemed to vanish through the open window into the warm night air. I realized all that stuff Robert and Obi-Wan Phillip told me about this moment was a load of crap. I didn't know what I was doing and dang sure didn't know what to do next. The darkness helped hide my embarrassment and how scared I really was.

About then I must have blacked out, because the next thing I knew my night of blissful torture was over and we were dropping Tone and Sandra off at their house.

As I told my side of the story to Phillip and Robert, they laughed and poked fun at me. They were still ribbing me the next day, as brothers and cousins do and as I deserved. Richard certainly told the story about his little cousin from Florida bombing out on his first date. Over the next few days Sandra would also kid me about how shy and inexperienced I was. She took great pains to detail how she could see my bright red face in the dark. I'm sure she also told everyone in Hale County that I didn't even kiss her.

It's easy for my present-day self to laugh at just how badly that awkward, embarrassing night turned out. All the events of the day and into the night, all of the buildup and anticipation and adrenaline . . . and still, I didn't get to kiss her. I almost wished it had been Robert or Obi-Wan Phillip in the back seat with Sandra—but then again, not!

I did not get my first kiss that night . . . but it was not a total loss. I *did* win the coin toss and *did* go on a date with Sandra—who will forever be known as the first girl I never kissed.

TO WALK IN THE PARK

By Kelley Rene

Leilani is on a mission. She'll do just about anything to gain her independence in this contemporary fiction that explores the complexities of family.

Kelley Rene is an award-winning author, speaker, and publisher who writes contemporary fiction to illustrate the mundane, the exhilarating, and even the stormy circumstances of life. Her three novellas, *Saving Sabine*, *Romanian Runaway*, and *Kamilah* are inspired by true events during her years in Europe. She is also the co-author of the international bestseller *Miracle Mindset: Finding Hope in the Chaos*.

Kelley resides in Panama City, Florida, with her husband and miniature Australian shepherd, Blossom. She loves to travel and meet new people, often the inspiration for her prose. When she's not scribbling insightful stories, you'll find her crocheting, kayaking, enjoying the beach, or cuddling a good book and cappuccino. Keep up with her at *kelleyrene.com* and on socials *@imkelleyrene*.

To Walk in the Park

THIS IS IT. Exactly what Leilani desires more than anything.

It's been three whole days since she stepped onto the streets of Washington, DC, having the greatest adventure of her life.

Finally, she's living *on her own.*

She gobbles down the cold fries she saved from lunch, just as the late September sun makes its descent behind the mile-high buildings.

Flowers capture the last rays in their upturned faces. They bloom in the nicely manicured streets, softening the pavement. Their bobbing heads remind Leilani of home. Her fingers itch to work the dirt around them, but they don't belong to her.

Her mother loves to garden. And so does Leilani.

The pair spends hours every summer clearing old mulch and decaying weeds. They replace dying bushes with rows of azaleas, liriope, and petunias. Color cascades throughout the front and back yards of their suburban home.

With a pang of guilt, she realizes her mother must garden alone now.

The moon pales against the backdrop of blues, purples, and pinks. Nights like this, they'd sit on the porch sipping lemonade. The kind her mom would make with the fresh lemons from the farmer's market down the street.

Her mouth is dry. Lemonade would taste so good!

Leilani studies the street signs, but the letters confuse her, dancing in the faint light like little fireflies. If she had a jar, she'd catch the fireflies and keep them next to her sleeping bag during the night. It'd be so much better than being in the pitch black alone.

Her feet throb from hours of meandering in and out of the city's sights. Her Vans, fresh from the box three days ago, rub all the wrong places. She hadn't even thought of bringing an extra pair. Much less socks.

She approaches an ornate fountain she admires each time she passes it. A small child climbs the slippery stone wall, and Leilani stops to watch. Perhaps the water would be soothing on her blisters? But an adult nearby yells and points to a sign, prompting the child to jump down to the pavement.

The familiar landmark orients her. Signs may flicker and dance, but every building, statue, and corner serves to guide her. She turns right onto 11th Street.

She smiles, silently praising herself for remembering the way. Last night, she'd raced right through the intersection before the little white man in the yellow box could disappear. Her mistake marched right along with her until they snaked around to the crowded, and very confusing, convention center. She wouldn't do that again.

As she rounds another corner, she sees a tall figure hovering over an ATM.

"Give me my money!" The man's voice echoes off the expansive concrete wall that anchors the dispenser.

Leilani halts, reluctant to get closer to the shadowed figure.

"I said gimme my money!" The man sways uneasily, just like Uncle Tommy last year on New Year's Eve when he showed up with breath like fire, clutching a glass bottle of something she'd never seen.

The sound of a fist connecting with metal and plastic shakes the air. She protects her ears with her hands.

Doesn't he know he needs a card and pin to make the machine spit out cash?

With knuckles edged in scarlet, the man throws another jab. "I. Want. My. Money!" He peppers the air with a handful of obscenities and threats.

Leilani cringes, but no one seems to care. Cars honk, tourists window-shop, and mobs of people wait at the street corners. All move at the same dull pace, unbothered by the commotion.

If she were here, her mother would say, "Those words tell me your mouth needs a good washin'."

Careful to look both ways, Leilani squeezes between two parked cars and staggers into the street. Once she is safely on the opposite sidewalk, she tests the security of the straps of her backpack over her shoulders.

A glance back at the deranged man with the bruised knuckles sends her bolting around the corner. She slows to a trot to catch her breath, but keeps going until she recognizes the familiar fast-food sign where they serve breakfast, lunch, and dinner. There's no one to tell her she can't eat hamburgers and fries more than once per day, so she slips inside for her evening meal.

The sun cowers behind translucent clouds as a blustery wind runs chilly fingers over Leilani's back. She hasn't slept a wink. The cardboard beneath her failed miserably as a mattress, and her bladder threatens to explode. Thankfully the alcove under the stairs offers solace from the dangers she imagines in the

DC nightlife. She burrows deeper into what has quickly become her most prized possession, the sleeping bag she swiped from the trunk of her brother's car. He's the reason she's here. He owes her that much.

She rubs the soft fabric over her cheek before unzipping the cozy sack down to her knees and wrestles out of it. It's so much softer than the one she'd been issued at camp this summer. Something putrid floats in with the wind. *Pew-ie!* She pulls an arm against her nose. It helps—a little.

A quick trot to an overgrown bush adjacent to the building shields her from street view. She steps around the shrub to look for anyone who might be watching before tucking herself behind the foliage once more, wiggling down her yoga pants, and squatting over a tuft of weeds.

What would her mother think?

Her poor mother. She's probably crying and crying.

The past few days have challenged Leilani more than she expected. Every movement, every sound, every thought culminates in doubt, casting her thoughts into a chasm of fear she'd never known. But something deep within her— something she doesn't understand—says her fear is not an enemy. It's an ally generating the energy she needs to survive.

Still, the thought of her frightened mother sneaks into her thoughts and spars with the accomplishment she feels swelling in her chest. She *is* doing it. She's living on her own.

Warmth runs down her thigh and soaks her leggings. "Ugh," she groans. Being on her own like this has some drawbacks.

"Oh well, they'll dry."

A quick dance shimmies her wet bottoms over her hips. As she smooths the waistband, she notices a face staring back at her from a pile of flyers on the ground nearby.

Her face.

She shakes the soaked paper off her sneaker, along with the leftover remorse for her mother's worry, and snatches up one of the pages least touched by tinkle. Her photo, taken months ago at her Granny's funeral, sits under a title that reads, "MISSING! Leilani Elizabeth Fuller (Autistic)."

She huffs and scuttles back to safety under the staircase. Why must they always attach *autistic* to her name? It's not like it's typed on her birth certificate like that. She knows because she read it once when her mom was organizing her important files.

Snuggled back into the sleeping bag, she holds the paper close to her face and squints to read the paragraph under the photo.

"I haven't disappeared. I'm right here," she announces, as if the person who designed the poster could hear her. Right here, in the city. Exactly where they'd said she couldn't go. Where they'd said she wasn't safe.

She crumples the paper, crams it under the balled-up sweatshirt she uses as a pillow, and snuggles deeper into the comfort of the sleep sack.

The week hasn't been too bad. Pride in her accomplishment swells again.

They said she couldn't live on her own. But she walked right up to a car in the snail lot, just like Daddy did every morning when she and Mom dropped him off at the ride-share conveniently located at the freeway exit for his commute into the city. "I choose a car with a driver dressed in a suit and a nice smile," Daddy said once. She remembers what he tells her. Even when he thinks she isn't listening.

"I've lived on my own for four days." She speaks quietly, puffing out her chest. Saying it aloud makes it real, somehow.

"I'm so proud of you!" Leilani hears her mother's voice in her head, although her mother is probably not thinking that now. But her family *will* see how well she can do on her own.

Footsteps silence her thoughts and turn her attention back to her surroundings. Frail morning light casts a pale halo around an ominous shadow as it descends the metal staircase that—up to now—felt like a turret soaring above her makeshift, personal castle.

Footfalls echo and ricochet around her concrete haven.

Her resolve crumbles. She holds her breath, praying not to be found. The sleeping bag presses against her nose. It filters the horrid smells that are brewing in the morning air.

The low growl of a dog nearby sends her heart into overdrive. If the stranger doesn't notice her, the mongrel certainly will.

The footsteps change from a metallic echo to a dull scuffling as the shadowed person steps from the staircase down onto the pavement.

She counts to twenty, giving the stranger time to disappear. But something moves nearby, uncomfortably close. A bass drum pounds in her chest. Ignoring it, she flings the sleeping bag off.

An older man with scraggly hair hunches in the corner, rifling through her backpack, stuffing his pockets with her belongings.

Her fear turns indignant. "Hey!"

The short-haired white mutt barks at her in reply, thin legs bouncing off the sidewalk just outside the concrete opening to her hiding place.

The man glances her direction.

"Leave my stuff alone!" Leilani jumps up, and her forehead collides with a steel rung overhead. Warm liquid spills down her face into her hands. The thump in her chest now pounds in her head.

The dog's bark, aimed at the thief, morphs into a low growl.

The man drops her pack and steps away, watching his canine foe with a wary expression.

"Get out of here!" With both palms pressed against her temples, Leilani gives a feeble shout, but the man is already making his escape around the staircase.

She drops to the ground and searches the pockets of her pack. Her cash and cellphone are missing. "No! No! No!"

The dog whimpers as it creeps closer. Its snout nudges and explores her elbow.

"Go away!" The last thing she wants is attention.

Fear and anger choke out her earlier feelings of pride. How dumb of her to think she could do this on her own. *Dumb! Dumb! Dumb!*

The dog howls, turns round and round until finally sitting at her feet with an air of purpose.

"Hush." Leilani hisses and swats a hand at the intruder, but the mutt doesn't budge. His tender eyes stare at her with determination. The black and brown blotches in his fur remind Leilani of her favorite houndstooth jacket. "Dog, you can't stay with me."

Even as she says the words, calm settles over her. It might be nice having a companion around. He wears no collar and seems rather infatuated with her. He's not a good listener, but what guy ever is?

Her mother's voice makes the joke in her thoughts, and Leilani wonders why her dad isn't a better listener.

Her vision blurs.

She dabs the sleeve of her thin down jacket at the moisture in her eyes. She winces at unexpected pain. When she pulls it away, a thin smear of blood from her face stains the fabric.

The dog whimpers, as if in sympathy. He lifts a front leg toward her.

"I never had a pet." She reaches over to shake his outstretched paw. "I'm Leilani. It's nice to meet you." She pauses to consider his appearance. "You look like a Spots."

He wags his tail, as if he agrees with the name.

She dabs at her forehead until the last trickle disappears, eyes closed against the discomfort.

With a growl, the dog leaps to all fours.

"What'cha got here?" Another man's voice!

Leilani twirls around at the sound. Once again, she collides with the metal railing and gasps at the impact.

"Careful, I don't want to hurt you." The man, balding and silver-haired, stares at her, holding out a hand as if in entreaty.

She glances away. "What do you want?" Her valuables are already gone. But he doesn't know that.

Her feet rock from side to side, absorbing the tremors spreading up her arms and into her chest. Fresh blood oozes down her forehead for the second time that morning, draining the will to fight from her.

The morning sunbeams highlight something poking against the man's right coat pocket, where his hand is hidden. It could be a gun, but she doesn't think so. He's more like a grandpa playing cops and robbers with his grandkids than a mean old criminal.

Spots takes three quick steps and halts partway between Leilani and the would-be robber. His growl revs like her daddy's motorcycle the time Mom let him take her for a ride around the block.

The man's mouth tightens. "Give me the sleeping bag, and I'll be on my way."

He's tired and worn and Leilani wants to give it to him. But how will *she* stay warm?

Spots takes another step forward as his growl shifts into an open-throttled, vicious snarl that shoots through her like electricity.

The man raises the corner of his jacket at her. "Toss it here or the pup's gonna get it."

She flinches and shuffles backward, careful not to go too far so she doesn't hit the back of her head on the overhang. "You can have it."

The man snatches a corner of the sleeping bag and balls it up into his arms. In a flash, he's gone, a trail of fabric billowing behind him.

Spots barks and growls like a mad dog.

Leilani presses a palm against her head and steps into the blustery morning.

Spots tears after the man, chasing him into the park across the street.

Now she's alone again. She hunkers down in the shadow of the staircase. Without the sleeping bag, she's already feeling the chill. Rocking side to side comforts Leilani's nerves, and she settles into the calm of the rhythm.

Spots rounds the staircase and plops down at her feet as if this is part of his normal routine.

She lets out a breath she didn't realize she'd been holding.

His tail thumps against a tattered pamphlet on the pavement for the *National Museum of Women in the Arts*.

She grabs the leaflet and studies it. "Where did this come from? It's exactly what I've been looking for."

Leilani stuffs it into her backpack, her one remaining belonging. She hoists the bag over her shoulder and steps out of her hiding place and glances back at Spots. "Are you coming?"

Dark clouds loom overhead as Leilani and Spots approach the McDonald's where she's enjoyed breakfast, lunch, and dinner every day since she arrived. "Stay here," she instructs the dog. Leilani likes the way the police officer smiles at her and says, "Good morning," "Good afternoon," and "Good evening," but today, the woman behind the badge points out the window towards the dog. "You've made a new friend."

She smiles and nods. "That's Spots."

A man and woman sporting matching Commanders ball caps are sitting near the window at Leilani's usual table.

It's okay, she tells herself. She doesn't have money to buy food today. Poor Spots. She wonders for the first time when he's eaten last. Her body rocks back and forth, back and forth, relieved the place isn't crowded. It feels nice. Maybe she and her mom can come here together, one day.

"Looks like you had a little accident."

Leilani immediately thinks of the tinkle that's long dried on her pants. She wrinkles her nose, embarrassed her clothes must smell like putrid fish. But the police officer points to her forehead.

Leilani runs her fingers above her eyebrows and flinches when she touches the gash.

She dismisses the pain and takes a step closer to the nice police lady, holding out the pamphlet. "Can you give me directions?"

The policewoman eyes the material. "Sweetie, the museum's right there." She points across the street.

Leilani pushes the glass door open for a better view of a structure she's passed numerous times during her explorations. Several rows of scaffolding encapsulate the building, shielding it against the early fall wind.

"It's closed for renovations." The woman shrugs, stating the fact as if anticipating the question.

Leilani murmurs "Thank you," and lets the door close behind her, ending their conversation.

Spots inches toward her and nuzzles her hand as if understanding her disappointment. He tilts his nose to the sky, bays as if announcing ownership of the area, then nestles at her feet.

She sighs, staring at the closed museum. "Looks like I won't get to see the artwork."

At summer camp last June, Leilani didn't like her itchy sleeping bag. She didn't like the food or having to be around so many excited people. But she loved painting classes with Ms. Tringa, the art teacher.

The memory is vivid. If Leilani closes her eyes, she can still smell the plastic scent of the acrylics.

"My favorite part of visiting Washington DC is meandering through the National Museum of Women in the Arts," Ms. Tringa says as her hand guides Leilani's steady strokes onto a prepared canvas. In her very first portrait, Leilani delicately paints bright blue eyes surrounded by pale porcelain skin just like Ms. Tringa's. No one recognizes the art teacher in the canvas, but Leilani trusts if she practices enough, they will someday.

Ms. Tringa knows everything about artwork.

Leilani isn't sure how to meander, but she leaves camp with a longing to see all of Ms. Tringa's favorites in the museum. She wants to learn everything about art, just like her teacher.

Now she is here, but the museum is closed.

Leilani drops to the pavement and presses her back against the wall of the building behind her, facing the structure. Cupping her hands around her eyes and squinting, she examines the maze of boards, poles, and metal rungs that hide the museum's sturdy facade.

Stroking the velvety ears of the little dog, she says, "It's like when my father cleans the gutters. Usually he climbs a ladder, but sometimes he sets two ladders side by side and puts a 2x4 across the top so he can reach more places. Then he balances himself on a plastic step stool on top of the board." She grins. "Whoo! My mother gets so mad at him when he does that. She yells, 'Get down from that contraption before you break your fool neck.' And he laughs and says he loves her and she worries too much."

Leilani looks at the scaffolding again. The levels are wider than a 2x4. Lots wider.

"Spots, stay here."

He cocks his head and lies down, resting his chin between his front paws.

She crosses the street when the little white man appears in the yellow box.

The metal feels cold when Leilani reaches for the first rung of scaffolding. She's come too far to turn back now without at least peeking into the museum.

The first window she reaches is covered in thick paper, so she eases herself along the wood, carefully holding onto the vertical rise in the scaffolding, until she reaches a second archway. It's also papered over, but the tier above appears to have uncovered, unprotected windows.

By shimmying up a pole, Leilani is able to hoist herself onto the next layer of wood. The breeze picks up, rustling the leaves on nearby shade trees and wafting the smell of French fries from the restaurant across the street. She tugs at her sleeve that twisted in the climb and tries to ignore her rumbling stomach.

The contraption sways under her jerky motions. She freezes, holding her breath, until it steadies. No wonder Mom gets mad at Daddy when he cleans the gutters! She repositions her hands carefully.

A shrill whistle pierces the air, and a couple of cars honk.

Leilani looks down.

"Hey! You shouldn't be up there!" The police lady stands in the middle of the street, waving to her.

Leilani tries to wave back, but the scaffolding moves again, and she quickly hooks her elbow around the pole next to her. It's farther from the ground than she thought it would be.

Now that she's braced, Leilani smiles and waves back.

The officer blows her whistle again and holds one gloved hand out to keep the traffic from continuing along the street.

She's the nicest police lady Leilani has ever met. Maybe they can give her one of Mom's sweet treats gift baskets for Christmas this year.

Leilani makes a mental note to ask Mom when she's back home.

The windows on this floor are dirty, but clear enough to see through. She peers in, giddy with excitement.

Two women, standing with their backs to her, stare at a painting she can't identify. How did they get in the building?

A siren wails in the distance. She flinches.

Intent on getting a look at the artwork, she tilts one direction, then the other. If only the two ladies would step just a little to the side, she could see much better.

One of them, wearing a dark blue business suit, points to the upper right corner of the ornate frame. Her body moves with the circular motion of her arm.

Surely, they wouldn't mind scooting over for Leilani.

She taps on the window with one finger, but the women continue in conversation.

"Hello?" she calls. Gently, she knocks with her knuckles, careful not to bang so hard the glass breaks.

From the street below, a siren wails. It's impossible for them to hear her, but they might hear that!

A longer blast of a siren reverberates in the brick canyon of downtown buildings. Leilani whimpers, protecting her ears with her cupped hands.

The woman in the navy suit turns and screams.

Leilani takes a startled step backward, but her foot wobbles and shifts the board beneath her. Her body twists as she desperately tries to stabilize her balance. Her hands swing away from her ears toward the closest pole, but she's not fast enough.

She falls lengthwise onto an ancient branch of a nearby tree. Bark scrapes against her cheek, and her feet flail in the air below the limb.

She squinches her eyes shut so she doesn't have to watch the ground bounce closer, then farther, then closer again. Her breath rushes in and out of her chest in giant gasps.

Finally, the bobbing stops, and she opens her eyes.

The police officer, face tilted up, waves both arms overhead, like people always do at summer beach concerts. She yells something, but Leilani can't hear it over the roaring in her own ears.

A fire truck stops below her. Several firefighters trot back and forth. At least the siren has stopped its horrible wailing.

A small crowd has gathered on the sidewalk, but the emergency personnel won't let them get too close.

Spots sits in front of the burger place where she'd left him, but now a leash connects him to the tired grandpa who stole the sleeping bag. The man leans against the building with one foot propped on the wall, leisurely watching the commotion. First, he stole her sleeping bag, now her new dog?

"Hey!" She yells at him from the tree. She doesn't dare let go.

With a metallic screech, an oversized white bucket containing one of the firefighters arises above the truck and slowly glides closer to her.

"Well, hello there." The first responder smiles when he calls to her, as calm and casual as if he rescues women in trees every day.

Leilani glances between the firefighter and the crowd forming on the street.

An ambulance idles next to the firetruck, and two paramedics stand, identically posed with feet braced apart and arms akimbo, in front of their vehicle. Both stare up at her. A man with a big camera records a woman speaking into a microphone. She turns and points the microphone toward the police lady.

Leilani wonders what they're saying. Are they waiting for her to fall? To fail?

But she's already failed.

Her arms start to shake. She buries her face against the unyielding tree branch while tears leak from her eyes.

"Beautiful day to hang out in a tree." The bucket carrying the fireman stops next to Leilani. He smells like her dad on Saturdays after mowing the lawn. "Do you plan to stay out here all day or are you ready to come down from your perch?"

Hours later, Leilani lounges in her favorite spot on the sofa, snuggling in her favorite cotton blanket. Her tummy rumbles in satisfaction, filled with a huge plate of lasagna, salad, and toasted butter bread—her favorite meal.

Her father and mother saunter into the family room.

"We need to talk." He settles into his recliner, clicking off the television with a wave of the remote.

Her mom sits on the other end of the couch, one foot tucked under her bottom, facing Leilani.

Here comes the lecture she's been waiting for. Dreading.

"I have to say. . ." Her father steeples his fingers. His voice is quiet, his cadence slow, as he seems to choose his words with care. "I'm proud of you."

Leilani presses her brows together. Not what she expected to hear.

"This week was hard, Leilani." Her mother puffs out a breath.

She nods in agreement. It *has* been hard. She went to DC with one goal in mind. Peeking into a window of the National Museum of Women in the Arts does not qualify as accomplishing that goal.

Her mother glances at her, then looks down. "I've never been more scared in my life, thinking of you all alone in the city."

"My little girl all alone in the big city." Her dad tag-teams smoothly, as if he and Mom rehearse all their responses.

Leilani moves to protest, but he raises both palms to stop her.

"I know. I know. You're not a little girl." He suddenly looks deflated, sad. "That's where your mom and I go awry. We struggle to see you for the mature woman that you're growing into."

She swallows, feeling a cold hard lump in her throat.

He wrings his hands together, just like she's seen him do many times before. "But you shouldn't have left like you did."

"I—" Leilani tries to interrupt, to force words past the boulder in her throat, but his raised palms stop her again.

"I get it. You knew if you asked, we would say 'No.'"

"I did ask." Leilani says the words quietly, thankful he doesn't interject. "I asked, and Mom said she couldn't take me." Leilani shoots a glance at her mother. "I overheard Jason say I'd never be able to live on my own. I decided to prove him wrong."

Her mother's lip trembles, and she catches it with her teeth.

Leilani touches the bandage the paramedics put on her forehead. "I guess I owe him a sleeping bag."

"Leilani." A flare kindles in her mother's eyes. "Your brother was wrong to say that. But you scared me to death!"

Now it's Leilani's turn to raise her palms in protest. "Mom, it was not my intention to frighten you. But I'm not a child. I *can* leave the house without you and do it safely." She shoves the irony of her words away and continues, determined. "You've always said I have a destiny. That God made me on purpose, with purpose."

Her father clears his throat but doesn't say anything, just folds his arms across his chest.

Leilani pulls the dogeared flyer from under the blanket and smooths out the creases. "I know I'm autistic. I've heard you say that too, over and over, through the years. I *know* I'm different. And I *know* you want to protect me. But I'm twenty-two years old. What young adult *doesn't* say and do stupid stuff?"

Her mother throws her arms into the air. "Stupid stuff? Trying to break into a museum isn't stupid, it's criminal."

"I wasn't trying to break in. I just wanted to see a painting. Any painting. I had come so far not to see *something* in the museum."

"Why didn't you go through the front door?" The fire in her mother's eyes shoots accusations at Leilani like darts.

She wants to retreat, run into her room, and sit in the dark. Instead she shoots up from the sofa and presses her hands shoulder height, allowing them to fling and flip outward, over and over again, fighting the tense air, trying to calm her anxiety.

"The police officer said it was closed. And I saw the scaffolding around the building. I didn't bother to check the front door."

The palms of her hands continue to flap wildly at her shoulders, their rhythm strangely soothing. Every day she works to hide her stimming. She wants so much to be normal. But now she doesn't care. If her mother insists on labeling her, why try to mask it?

"Leilani, there's no need to shout." Her father relaxes his arms and lets them fall to his sides.

"I'm not shouting!" Even as she says the words, she forces herself to speak slowly, more quietly. "I'm tired of hearing I'm autistic like it's some kind of disease." She takes a deep breath. "I have a purpose, a destiny. You told me that."

Her father meets her gaze and she wills herself not to look away. Finally, he glances at her mother, and then at the tips of his shoes.

When neither parent objects, she continues with more courage and conviction. "I want the freedom to wake up when I want. I want the freedom to walk in the park when I want. I want the freedom to live my own life." She sits down, no longer feeling the compulsion to stim, although the room is still thick with tension.

She folds her arms and juts out her chin. "And I want my own place."

The doorbell rings.

Leilani avoids her mother's gaze as her father shuffles from the room.

She strains her ears but can't make out any words from her father's mumbled conversation in the foyer. The front door closes with a muted thump, while scrabbling sounds and jingling noises punctuate the masculine voices.

"Easy, now!" A man laughs, and a happy, high-pitched yip answers him.

Leilani's trusty city companion barrels into the living room, tail wagging and tongue lolling.

She hops off the sofa, squealing with delight. "Spots!"

The dog jumps into her arms, whimpering with the effort to lick every inch of her face and fingers.

"How'd you get here?"

Her father struts in, followed by a man Leilani recognizes. She releases Spots, absorbing the unexpected presence of the silver-haired stranger.

"Leilani, this is Billy Mason." Her dad smiles at Leilani.

She stiffens, glaring as her mother reaches over to shake the newcomer's hand. When he extends his palm toward Leilani, she leaves it dangling midair.

"Talk about criminal behavior." Leilani eyes the man, scowling. "You stole my brother's sleeping bag."

Her mother's expression falls.

"Mr. Mason is a private detective." Her dad scratches the back of his neck, clearly uncomfortable. "I hired him to find you."

Leilani and her mother gasp in unison.

"You–What?" Leilani stares at her father, betrayal curdling the lasagna in her tummy.

He folds his arms over his chest, massaging his biceps. "My mind imagined the worst."

"So he steals her sleeping bag?" Her mother's eyebrows rise with indignation.

"Once I knew she was safe, I told him to test her to see how she'd handle a setback."

"Unbelievable!" Mom tosses her head and storms from the room. Cabinets slam in the kitchen, then she reappears in the doorway. "I've been losing my mind all week. Printing flyers. Organizing the neighbors to distribute them. Praying. Crying. You watched me suffer and didn't tell me where she was?"

Her dad crosses the room to her. "I'm sorry." He places a hand on her shoulder.

She shies away from his touch.

"Jody, I knew you'd race to the city for her." He waits, as if hoping her boiling anger will dissipate. "I wanted to see how she'd handle herself."

"Let's see. How did she do?" Her face flushes. "She lost her phone and her cash. She ate nothing but hamburgers all week. She climbed the scaffolding to the third floor of a museum, got caught in a tree, and had to be rescued by the fire department."

Silence.

Leilani purses her lips. "In my defense, someone stole my phone and cash. I didn't lose them. And I had sausage biscuits for breakfast."

Her mother drops her face into her palms and slinks from the room again.

Mr. Mason winces, looking sheepish and embarrassed. "I paid a homeless guy five bucks to rifle through your bag." He pulls a cell phone from his jacket and hands it out to her. "I didn't realize he made off with your cash. Tell me how much, and I'll reimburse you. I've got your brother's sleeping bag in my truck."

"That still doesn't explain about Spots." Leilani reaches down to pick up the dog lying at her feet. She nuzzles his nose with her own.

He gives a tentative lick, then squirms against her until she lets him slide to the floor.

She glances at Mr. Mason, waiting for an explanation.

His mouth twists as if he's chewing words before spitting them out. "He's my huntin' hound. Your dad gave me one of your socks, and he tracked you down. That female police officer patrols the area and spotted you at the burger joint. She was keeping an eye on you 'cauz of the posters."

Leilani's mother bangs another cabinet door in the kitchen. "She could have contacted us."

Dad snorts. "She did."

An extra-loud slam from the kitchen, followed by rattling dishes, conveys Mom's opinion on that fact.

He met Leilani's gaze and gave a rueful shrug.

Mr. Mason shoves his hands into his pockets, lifting his shoulders like a turtle pulling its head into its shell. "Anyway. With that as the starting point, he led me right to you. Then I told him to guard you, he's good at that too."

"But he growled and scared you away this morning." Leilani plants her hands on her hips, contemplating the scenario. She pokes a pointer at him. "He wouldn't snarl at his owner."

Spots cocks his head, wagging his tail from his post at the girl's feet. But when Billy Mason tucks a hand in his jacket pocket and points it at the dog, Spots bolts onto all four paws and bares his teeth, reenacting the scene from earlier that morning. "Grrrrrr!" Billy growls back, and the pair perform a rousing dance of prolonged snarling, yipping, and hopping in and out of an invisible circle.

Billy snaps his finger, transforming Spots into a focused companion once more who drops on his haunches at the man's feet. The old man turns back to Leilani. "He's trained to play fight. If I had run out of the room, he would've chased me until I gave him the signal."

No one says a word, including Leilani who stares at the two mesmerized.

"I'll be on my way." Mr. Mason whistles as he turns toward the foyer. Spots hops up with a little whine and glances at Leilani. "Come on now," the man says, and the dog disappears after his owner around the corner.

On the sofa, Leilani's father pulls her against his chest and smothers her in a hug. "Sweetie, we're so glad you're home, and so very glad you're safe."

Her mother appears through the kitchen door. Splotches pepper her face, and she rubs her sleeve over her runny nose. She joins the hug, wrapping her arms around them both. "Yes, it's great to have you back home, Leilani. I promise to take you to the museum this weekend."

Leilani squeezes her parents, appreciating the embrace, then pulls away. "Mom, Dad, I'm serious. I want my own place."

Her mother splutters, dashing away tears.

Leilani presses. "It isn't because I don't love you. I want to make my own way in this world. I want to spread my wings and fly."

Her dad draws in a weighty breath. "You might be surprised to hear your mom and I have talked this over at length." He pats her shoulder. "We have a surprise for you. It's not quite ready, but—"

Leilani presses her hands together to stifle the onset of stimming.

Sheer joy spreads across her father's face. "We bought a condo across from your favorite park in town. We're finalizing the renovations, but it's yours to live in as long as you want."

"Seriously?" Leilani whoops and hollers, jumping up and down. "I'll be able to walk in the park any time I want to."

She twirls in the center of the living room, and her parents laugh.

Her dad puts an arm around his wife. Their faces glow with delight.

"Yes, you can walk in the park any time you want to, sweetie." He nods in emphasis.

Leilani smiles. Yesterday, she was wrong. This . . .*This* is exactly what she desires, more than anything. The greatest adventure of her life is, finally, about to begin.

THE GREATEST GIFT

By Gary Baker

In this work of fantasy, Anne-Elise sits at the crux of a decision. Will she accept the challenges that await her and embrace a new gift or run from the fear that threatens to overtake her?

Gary Baker lives in central Georgia with his wife, Pam, and Petra, the family dog. He's been writing in his spare time since leaving the U. S. Navy in 1989, and devotes most of his free time to writing since his retirement as an engineer in 2022.

The Greatest Gift

ANNE-ELISE SAT in the garden enjoying the cool afternoon. With her eyes closed, she brushed her fingers back and forth across the surface of the bench beside her. It was polished granite. Or it might have been quartz. She could never remember. Whatever the material, it was smooth and surprisingly comfortable. She came here often and simply sat, shaded by the tall oak nearby.

In the background, the wind blew through the trees, and she felt the rhythm of the branches as they swayed back and forth. Leaves shook in the breeze, rustling lightly. A robin called from a nearby branch. Further away, a small stream bubbled and foamed as the water fell and rose against stones long washed clean. A twig snapped nearby. Clothing whispered and sandals padded on the path, increasing in volume as someone approached.

"Practicing your breathing, I see." Andrew sat next to her. Anne-Elise opened her eyes, just a peek, and watched as he settled himself on the bench, his robes gathered gracefully around him. She often wondered how he made such simple movements seem elegant. He leaned back, his own eyes now closed to enjoy the sounds of the day.

"Not really." A light smile formed on her lips.

"A pity," he said. "It's an important skill. Most people do it their entire lives."

Anne-Elise giggled as she turned to look at him.

He opened his eyes and met her gaze. He returned her smile as he always did, white teeth shining, a kind sparkle in his eyes. His hair was perfectly arranged, combed back from the forehead, with a touch of gray at the temples that spoke not of age but of wisdom. Anne-Elise had often wondered how old he was, though she had never asked. It seemed impolite somehow.

Andrew faced her. He placed a hand on the open space between them and Anne-Elise reached out in return. His touch seemed unusually cool today but not uncomfortably so.

Her body was changing. The birthing time approached. She often felt too hot now and even minor tasks left her clammy with sweat, so she frequently sought out the garden, which was always cool and pleasant. As cool and pleasant as the hand she now held.

"How are you feeling today?" Andrew's smile remained, but she could see the concern in his eyes.

Anne-Elise had seen that same look a few times, when she was feeling overly anxious or frightened or just plain mean. Each time he had told her the perfect thing to give her a measure of peace.

There were others around, of course. Other attendants. Others waiting as she was. She talked with them often, and that helped. But there was no one like Andrew. He was the oil on her troubled waters.

The day she arrived, she'd tried to project an appearance of calm determination. Inside she had never been so anxious. She had always been surrounded by the familiar, the routine, but everything here was different from what she knew. Frightening. She had been tempted to leave immediately and return home. The choice that led her here seemed more like a moment of insanity, a challenge that she could never overcome. At that moment she first saw Andrew walking toward her, hands neatly folded in his robe, smiling broadly.

He'd taken her hand and slowly led her to her new room, chatting about everything and nothing, telling her how happy he was to meet her. As they strolled through the grounds, he introduced her to the residence where she would spend the next nine months. He showed her the meditation rooms, the dining hall where they would take their simple meals, a room for light exercise though he confided that it saw little use. There was a chapel, of course, but instead of pews, it was filled with large pillows and comfortable chairs. And he introduced her to the others that had come, seeking rest and comfort until their time came. It had helped. She still had trouble sleeping that night, but that first meeting left her feeling hopeful.

Anne-Elise sighed. She would have liked to have been bright and cheerful, to have told him that she was fine and send him off to provide support for some other needy arrival . . . but that would have been worse than useless. In the past nine months, Andrew and Anne-Elise had shared everything. He knew her almost as well as she knew herself. He would know that she was being dishonest, and that would worry him even more.

"It's been rough these last few days." She turned away and lowered her head as though contemplating the slippers she wore daily. Her eyes burned with unwanted tears. She hated that feeling, that loss of control. She had already cried more in the last few months than she had in all the time before. It wasn't an enjoyable experience, especially when she knew there was more to come.

"Don't be afraid." Andrew slid closer to her and placed a hand gently on her shoulder. "You are safe here. You are loved."

"I don't feel like it." The first tear began its journey down the smoothness of her cheek.

"What do you feel like?" Andrew asked.

Her throat contracted, thick with mucus, making it difficult to speak. "I feel . . . tight."   Her voice was a hoarse whisper. "I feel like an apple shoved into a grape skin. Like there's a pressure all around me. It's difficult just moving. My arms and legs are so cramped, stiff . . ."

She paused there, her throat too clogged to pass more words. She closed her eyes tightly, as if she could stop the tears now flowing down her cheek and throat. Her hands shook and, try as she might, she could not still them.

"Just breathe." Andrew's voice was low and soothing. "Clear your mind and breathe."

Anne-Elise would have laughed if she could. How many times had Andrew repeated that simple phrase during her stay here? A dozen? A hundred? At different times the words had puzzled her, frustrated her, downright infuriated her. She had pushed him, yelled at him. At times she had struck him, though never with any real anger. It was impossible to get angry with him, despite his bull-headed persistence. And in the end, she had always relented, worn down by his still, small voice, and began to breathe. And then, as now, the worst began to pass.

"I have headaches," she continued, eyes still down. Her voice sounded choked and her nose ran freely. She hated that anyone should see her like this.

Soft fabric brushed against her hand, as Andrew passed the handkerchief he always carried. She had wondered about the habit when she first arrived. She had learned the reason quickly. Between her and his other charges, tears were a common occurrence. She dabbed her cheeks and wiped her nose.

"The sun seems too bright. Even the lights in the rooms are uncomfortable." Turning to him, she asked, "Does everyone feel like this?"

"To one extent or another." He looked up and she followed his gaze. The sky gleamed an azure blue, with light wisps of clouds moving steadily to the west. The ground was marked by patches of yellow and white where the sunlight passed through the leaves and branches above. Andrew ran his fingers along his collar, then looked down, biting his lip. "I guess my robes don't help, do they?"

"Not much." Anne-Elise managed a tiny smile and a chuckle that sounded more like a cough. Her brightened mood was short-lived, however.

Andrew's eyebrows furrowed as the frown reappeared.

She scuffed her toe in the dirt, watching a pattern form. She took a few deep breaths. "Is it too late to change my mind?"

Andrew turned slightly, facing the garden rather than looking directly at her. "The choice has always been yours, Anne-Elise." He steepled his fingers in his lap. "But you have to make it soon. You are very near your time. Be sure of your reasons."

"I'm frightened," she said quietly. "I don't know if I can go through with this."

"I know." Still looking at the garden, Andrew reached out and took her hand, squeezing it firmly now. "Frightened to go forward. Frightened to go back. I would do anything I could to take that fear away from you, but I can't. It's good to be a little afraid. Things are about to change whatever decision you make. Just don't let fear blind you to what you really want."

"And if I choose to leave now?" Anne-Elise rubbed her stomach with her other hand. "I see all of the others walking around, so happy about what is to come. What will they think of me? What will you think of me, Andrew?"

"I wouldn't be too sure that they are as confident as they seem." He turned toward her, a hint of sadness in those kind eyes. "We will think that your path lay elsewhere. You wouldn't be the first to leave, and you won't be the last. The only judgment you risk is that which you will put on yourself. Our love, my love, for you will never change."

Anne-Elise scooted herself close and hugged Andrew tightly, her whole body shaking. His neck and robe grew damp as sobs poured from her. As he held her close, gently stroking her back, she felt his tears on her shoulder. The tremors slowly eased but her tears continued to flow for several long minutes.

A powerful spasm grabbed her. She let out something between a groan and a whimper. Her body stiffened and her grip on Andrew became so tight that she feared he could scarcely breathe. They held each other like this for half a minute before her body relaxed and she slowly pulled away.

"Was that—?" She fisted her hands as she fought to master her fear.

"A contraction, yes." Andrew nodded.

A pair of orderlies in white jackets came along the garden path toward them as if summoned by magic. One pushed a gurney. Its wheels squeaked slightly as it rolled toward her.

Andrew placed his palm over her clasped fingers. "You must decide now. Do you wish to go home, or head to the birthing room?"

"I don't know!" Anne-Elise closed her eyes tightly and squeezed Andrew's hand again as hard as she could. Something wonderful and terrible was happening, and butterflies fluttered in her belly, her lungs, her mind.

She opened her eyes and looked at Andrew. "I need more time."

"Anne-Elise . . ." The priest placed his other hand on her shoulder. He met her gaze, and there was no worry or concern in his eyes. There was only reassurance. "You've been waiting to make this decision your entire life."

The orderlies brought the gurney to a stop a few steps away. They smiled but said nothing, just waited for her.

She looked back and forth between Andrew and the two men for a few seconds, breathing rapidly, listening to the rustling leaves, the bubbling brook, the cheerful robin. She finally turned to Andrew, meeting his gaze firmly.

"Take me to the birthing room," Anne-Elise said.
Andrew stood with a smile, his hand still in hers, and helped her to her feet. The two walked to the gurney. The orderlies lowered the rails and helped her aboard. When she was settled, they adjusted the gurney to full height and prepared to leave.

"What happens now?" Anne-Elise refused to relinquish her grip on Andrew's hand.

"Rejoice." Andrew smiled at her. "You are about to give the greatest gift that one person can give to another. The gift of life."

He bent down and kissed her on the forehead. He slowly released her hand and stepped back. The gurney begin to move, one man pushing as the other guided the conveyance along the path. As they turned a corner, Andrew smiled at her and waved. She gave a tired wave in return.

"Goodbye," she whispered.

It had been a long, hard labor. The tired woman had lost track of the minutes and hours, pushing and breathing, pushing and breathing. As the last contraction ended, she lay back, eyes closed, waiting for the next wave of pain. She felt coolness spread across her forehead as her husband wiped sweat away with a soft washcloth. She opened her eyes and saw him give an encouraging smile as he took her left hand in his.

"Be strong, Margaret," he said. "It will all be over soon."

She nodded and smiled in return. It was a brief gesture. Pain surged again and she lay back, taking deep breaths and counting to herself.

"The baby is crowning!" Her obstetrician's voice, cheerful and upbeat, sounded from the other side of a cloth barrier. Dr. Meyers had been in and out of her room for hours now, monitoring contractions and checking vitals. The labor had been long and difficult, and the doctor had even suggested a C-Section might be necessary since the mother-to-be was almost at the end of her strength. "One last push!"

She leaned forward in her bed, bearing down with all her might. Her husband's hand cradled her own, firm against the pressure. This was her last effort. If the baby did not come now—

"I have the baby!" Dr. Meyers announced. "It's a girl! A perfect baby girl."

Margaret lay back in her bed, completely exhausted, but joyful as well. Sleep beckoned, although she tried to fight it, holding fast to thoughts of her child. She wanted desperately to see this miracle, to hold her in her arms.

But she could not.

Her husband left her side. The nurses moved away to see to the newborn. She slowly drifted off, a satisfied smile on her face.

The back of the hospital bed shifted, tilting her upward and rousing her from her exhausted doze. A faint sound, like the bleating of a lamb, seemed to come from far away. Her throat was dry from labor and she had to concentrate to swallow. Her eyelids felt sticky. It took her several tries to open them, and a few more seconds elapsed before she could focus.

James sat in the bedside chair. He was smiling, but not at her. His gaze was fixed on the small bundle crying out from the tiny bassinet.

"James." She croaked his name, barely a whisper, but somehow he heard her over the squalling child. He looked at her, and his smile grew brighter. He lifted the baby into her waiting arms, then poured a cup of water. Bringing the cup to her lips, he helped ease the soreness in her throat is if knowing she would not remove either hand from cradling the tiny girl, even to drink.

"She's perfect." James reclaimed his seat. "She's strong and healthy, and feisty like her mother."

She nodded, barely hearing his words. As she rocked back and forth, the child began to settle and was soon asleep. She knew that wouldn't last. Very soon the child would awaken and need to be fed, and that was fine . . . but in this moment she was perfectly content. All was as it should be. There were no regrets from the past, no worries about the future. There were no pressing issues, no serious matters for consideration. There was only joy as she nestled the small life close to her.

"So, what's her name?" James leaned closer, grinning.

She chuckled. They'd held many discussions on the subject in the past few months. James had his preferences, and she had her own favorites. In the end, James had relented, saying the choice was hers. As usual.

They sat in comfortable silence for almost an hour before the child began to stir again. Within a few seconds, the sound of crying filled the room. Margaret knew that in the weeks and months to come she might resent that sound, for it would wake her in the night and interrupt rare moments of peace. But right now, the thin wails resonated like the song of a heavenly choir.

She could feel nothing but gratitude.

She and James had received the greatest gift there was, the gift of life. The gift of a child.

"Anne-Elise," Margaret said, caressing the tiny face. "Her name is Anne-Elise."

THE OLDE TOBACCO BULLION SHOPPE

By Luisa Kay Reyes

Day after day, Pierson, a recently divorced man, haggles over the price of gold, believing he'll soon be able to retire in Costa Rica. To his dismay, retirement stretches farther out of reach until in a subtle turn of events his perspective shifts.

Luisa Kay Reyes has had pieces featured in "The Raven Chronicles", "The Windmill", "The Foliate Oak", "The Eastern Iowa Review", and other literary magazines.

Her essay, "Thank You", is the winner of the April 2017 memoir contest of "The Dead Mule School Of Southern Literature". Her Christmas poem was a first place winner in the 16th Annual Stark County District Library Poetry Contest. Additionally, her essay "My Border Crossing" received a Pushcart Prize nomination from the Port Yonder Press. And two of her essays were nominated for the "Best of the Net" anthology with one of her essays recently being featured on "The Dirty Spoon" radio hour.

The Olde Tobacco Bullion Shoppe

PIERSON GLANCED AT the message from his attorney on his phone. No more waiting. The divorce had gone through. It was final. He was now a free man.

Although, free for what, he wasn't sure.

Such was the life for one of the last of the knuckle-dragging Cro-Magnon cavemen.

Pierson sighed. Nothing else he could do. Just keep at it. His divorce had set back his plans to retire to Costa Rica and sell margaritas on the beach by at least seven years.

Good thing the value of gold was up today. There would be plenty of customers wanting to hawk their valuables at the Olde Tobacco Bullion store he managed. With the precious metal predicted to go up even more later in the month, he had an opportunity to stock up on jewelry now which could be sold to the refinery at a premium. He'd earn a commission on each of the transactions. Maybe he could recoup some of the money he lost in the divorce settlement. If he played his cards just right, he'd get to Costa Rica before the nursing home beckoned.

Maybe.

"Good morning, Wilbur." Pierson stepped out of his car in front of the Olde Tobacco Bullion, not even five minutes late.

Tall, gray-haired Wilbur fidgeted near the door, his rolled-up newspaper under his arm. Judging from the impatient expression on his face, he wanted to take his usual seat at one of the worn-out chairs inside as soon as possible.

"I had some personal matters to attend to this morning, but I'll get the coffee going in just a minute." Pierson unlocked the door and held it open for the older man.

Silence was his only reply. And silence was the only response Pierson expected.

By the time warm brown liquid caffeine started flowing down his throat, Pierson relaxed a little. Out of habit, he gazed through the front window, cataloging the cars pulling into the shopping center. Theirs was not a high-end plaza, but neither was it low-rent. Whenever a faded, mud-ridden rattletrap pulled into the parking lot, Pierson knew he'd have a customer—someone down to their last dollar, hoping to make ends meet by selling their grandfather's antique watch, which might or might not be ensconced in a 24K gold case. But this car pulling up in front of his door stuck out. Not ritzy enough to be driven by one of the physicians or lawyers that constituted his wealthiest clientele ... but probably not a customer that might get him called into court.

A beauty stepped out of the vehicle. Long flowing dark hair framed perfect features and accentuated an hour-glass figure.

Mercy! Pierson straightened up and sucked in his gut. What cruel twist of fate could be bringing her here?

The bell rang as the door opened. She glanced around. Her gaze paused on Wilbur, sitting in his customary chair, reading his newspaper.

"Good morning." She offered a shy smile.

Silence ensued.

Pierson met her quizzical gaze. "Vietnam Vet."

Wilbur had never volunteered that information to him, of course. He'd deduced it from some of the ball caps Wilbur wore over the years.

"Oh!" She shot a furtive glance at the old man, then placed a single silver coin on top of the counter.

Pierson stifled a sigh. Silver was more valuable than nothing, but if she were hoping to make a decent sale today, it would be better for it to have been gold.

"I need money for tuna fish for my kitty cats." She bit her lip. "And some steaks for my mother and me would be good, too."

He examined the coin. Although high quality silver, even if he gave her the highest possible rate, it most assuredly would not suffice for steaks and tuna fish.

Her soft brown eyes held a lot of trust. And even his inner Cro-Magnon didn't want to let her down.

"Tell you what." He rubbed the back of his neck. "I can help with the cats and their tuna fish. How many cans do you need?"

She blinked twice and gave a half-shrug. "Well, I have six rescue kitties."

"Perfect! Wait right here." He headed to the back of the store and ransacked the cabinets in the break room. His wife— ex-wife, now—used to nag him to eat more healthily, and packed nutritious but unappetizing meals for months before declaring his diet a lost cause. He had immediately stashed the cans of tuna fish on a back shelf and promptly forgotten about them. Now he just needed to remember where they were.

He spotted dusty cans of tuna in the back corner of the upper shelf. He nearly crowed in triumph. Based on the number of neatly stacked cans, he had enough to feed a whole army of feral kitties.

For now, he would give the gal a can for each kitty for a total of six. With any luck, her cats would beg for another treat and she might request extra cans on another shopping trip to the Olde Tobacco Bullion.

"Take these." He tucked them into a plastic sack.

"Okay."

He opened the till and took out a couple bills. "And this is for your steaks."

It wasn't much, given the light weight of her silver coin. But the look of relief in her eyes spoke volumes.

"Oh, thank you!" She slipped the cash into her purse. "I've just lost my job as a music teacher. With summer vacation starting, it's tough to make ends meet before the next term begins. I might even be back next week!"

She sallied out of the store toward her car, waving farewell to Wilbur on the way.

Pierson glanced at the lone coin on the scale. He had misread it. A pang of agony hit his gut. He hadn't given her much, but he'd still overpaid her.

"Hang it all!" He dropped the coin into the inventory drawer. "I'm getting soft."

The corners of Wilbur's lips curved upward. He silently flipped to the next sheet and buried his head back down into the newspaper.

The next day, a plain sedan pulled up in front of the store. The license plate featured a blue flag and white saltire. A square-faced Scotsman jumped out and headed for the entrance.

Pierson grinned. He knew this customer with the vanity plate, a naturalized American citizen who still proudly boasted of the land of his birth.

"Angus!" Pierson leaned on the counter. "Good to see ya!"

"Aye, morning, Pierson!" Angus strode in. "Hullo Wilbur!" Angus gave a nod in Wilbur's direction, but didn't wait for an answer.

Sure enough, silence was the only greeting he got in return.

Angus placed a sturdy sack on the counter. Coins jingled softly. "I have here a bag full of one-ounce silver buffalo coins, if you'll let me have that there first strike gold eagle coin at twenty percent off."

Pierson chuckled. Angus may have become naturalized, but he was still a Scotsman when it came to buying and selling bullion. He poured the contents onto the glass top for a quick count and appraisal. "Sure, why not?"

After all, those one-ounce silver buffalo coins would sell quickly. They were so popular he could hardly keep them in stock.

He unlocked the cabinet and fetched the shiny gold eagle in its protective case. "Here. We'll call it an even trade."

"Good." Angus rubbed his hands with a satisfied smile. "Now, tell me why you didn't tell me the store was up for sale?"

Pierson coughed. "Well, it could be because I didn't know. What are you talking about?"

"Och, you haven't seen it!" Angus pulled up an advertisement on his cell phone.

Pierson squinted at the screen, then sucked in a breath. It would have been nice if the owners had apprised him of the matter personally. Or at least dropped hints about impending changes. Especially if it meant he'd be looking for another job soon.

"You know what this means." Angus tapped the phone. "It means one of those big chains will come in and take over."

Costa Rica suddenly felt much further away.

Although, he was a certified gemologist. Courtesy of his wife—ex-wife. That had to count for something even in today's job market.

He sagged against the counter, staring at the smooth glass surface.

A hush that didn't come from Wilbur alone lingered with a heavy weight throughout the length and breadth of the store.

"Let me look into it." Angus finally broke the mutual silence of everyone present. He put his prize into his pants pocket.

Pierson gave a rueful smile. Angus was ever the Scotsman. "Sure, why not?" He echoed his earlier words with a halfhearted shrug.

Angus hurried out of the store with the impetus of a man on a mission.

No telling what the wheeler-dealer might try, but Pierson was pretty certain this was a task too big for even Angus' money-making machinations.

Pierson took a deep breath, pondering the virtues of the good ol' days of Sparta in ancient Greece. All a man needed to do to make a living was go off to war and return home to be waited on by voluptuous serving maids. Much simpler and more satisfying than staring at accounts on the computer screen all day. Ah! Ancient Sparta—what a life.

The next week, a wave of bank failures created a stir in the store. Suddenly everyone wanted to buy bullion to safeguard their earnings.

Pierson could hardly keep up with all of the customers milling in and out. In spite of ample air conditioning in The Olde Tobacco Bullion Shoppe, beads of sweat formed on his forehead and streamed down his neck. He tried to wipe the perspiration off as quickly as he could, but it flowed out as rapidly as the frantic customers.

When the morning rush finally subsided a bit, he ducked outside to take a whiff or two of his cigar. *Whew!* It felt good to relax for a while, although, he did have to admit, these bank failures equaled profits for his business.

The lull didn't last long. State Senator McFarrell, a tall man in a sharp business suit approached the store, a hail-fellow-well-met smile on his face. "If you keep that up, you'll kill yourself before you make it to Costa Rica."

"Just being true to the name of the establishment. We can't call it 'The Olde Tobacco Store' for nothing." Pierson allowed the politician to shake his hand with the double grip of long acquaintance.

Although not in the same graduating class, some of their high school years at The Academy had overlapped. McFarrell, of course, had been popular, while Pierson was shunned—except during football season. These days the state senator considered him an old school chum. And a potential voter.

The state senator's practiced smile widened. "I'm helping sponsor the Liberty Banquet this year, and I was hoping you'd have some Liberty Bell coins I could give to some of the top donors."

Pierson took another puff of cigar, savoring the spicy wood scent. "They've just about cleared me out, what with the bank failures and all—"

"Darn liberals!" McFarrell snorted. "Trying to rush this country into wrack and ruin quicker than the blink of an eye when a streak of lightning strikes. Not to mention their fanatical attachment for a socialist dictatorship that nobody can afford to pay for. Before you know it, they'll have us all bowing down to Karl Marx and wearing turbans on our heads!"

Yup, McFarrell hadn't changed all right.

Pierson stubbed out his cigar and opened the door with an ushering gesture. "Come on in. I think I saved some A-mark silver Life, Liberty, and Happiness Liberty Bell coins in the back. Just in case you stopped by."

"Good morning, Wilbur!" McFarrell, a true politician to the core, greeted the old man with enthusiasm.

Silence, of course, was his response.

Undeterred, McFarrell pointed at the newspaper. "If you look at the bottom of the opinion page, the state house columnist has a nice article on the bill I'm sponsoring to promote patriotism in our schools."

Wilbur nodded his head and turned the page in the same lackadaisical manner that he always employed.

McFarrell, of course, took the motion as an indication of approval for the work he was doing. "Got to keep those liberals at bay, you know. Keep them from corrupting our youth."

Liberals, liberals, liberals. Everything was always the fault of the liberals, where McFarrell was concerned.

Pierson shook his head as he peered into the tall safe in the back which held some of the more valuable items. He'd definitely reserved some Liberty Bell coins for McFarrell—now his task was to find them in the chaos that the crazy morning's rush had precipitated. *Aha!* Third row in the back. Pierson removed the velvet-covered tray that held the coins and placed it atop the glass counter in front of McFarrell.

"Marvelous! I'll take them all." McFarrell's eyes glinted like the coins, which shone like new underneath the store lights.

Pierson tallied the amount and waited while McFarrell swiped his credit card without raising an eyebrow at the total. Must be nice to be raised in a family with an extensive—and highly lucrative—real estate business. Using mental math, he calculated his commission, a standard percentage of every sale. A few more customers like McFarrell, and he'd have a decent deposit for his Costa Rica fund.

He glanced at the parking lot, still devoid of cars. The morning rush had been a fluke, after all. Who was he kidding? The state senator's personal agenda was the only reason he'd paid top dollar like that. Everyone else was just trying to scrape by.

"Now, tell me." McFarrell leaned across the counter, his voice low and confidential. "The homecoming queen at Cinder Valley High School. The one who was just crowned last week, petite little cheerleader with blonde hair. I hear she's your niece, isn't she?"

Pierson stiffened, drawing himself up to his full height. "Yes."

He knew McFarrell's reputation, of course. Disbelieved it, perhaps, knowing the liberals always maligned conservative politicians, and he wanted to give his old schoolmate the benefit of the doubt. But awareness stabbed him now.

The state senator smiled. "You know, I dated a girl from County High last year. And the year before, I dated a girl from Hilltop High School."

Pierson narrowed his eyes, pointedly letting his glance sweep over McFarrell's paunchy physique and graying hair. The man was old enough to be those girls' father with more than a few years left over.

McFarrell winked. "How about putting in a good word for me with your—"

"Back off!" Pierson packed his voice with force and fierceness summoned directly from his younger days in the Marine Corps.

"Hey, take it easy. I treat my girls right!" The politician eased back, his arms open in a nothing-to-see-here shrug, his face wide with a smarmy leer.

"I said, back off!" Pierson clenched his fists. The muscles in his arms bulged, rippling with a trained strength he didn't know they still possessed.

McFarrell dropped an f-bomb, scooped his coins off the counter, and bolted out of the store. One of the Liberty Bells slipped from his grasp when he shoved the door open, and it skittered across the floor, but he left it behind as he exited The Old Tobacco Bullion Shoppe without a backward glance.

"Don't show your face again, pervert!" Pierson pounded the countertop, wishing he could connect with the politician's head. Or something lower.

The glass shattered.

Wilbur's eyebrows rose. Wordlessly, he turned the page in his newspaper.

Pierson fished a postcard from the wrecked display case. A scenic sun-filled view in Costa Rica, normally it rested on the counter beside his computer screen.

Ah! Costa Rica.

Maybe his niece could come with him. He could look out for her. Keep her out of the clutches of creeps like McFarrell.

But right now, he had to gather the shards of glass he had just sent flying all over the place. Then see about getting the counter fixed.

"Guess I better figure out how to explain all this to my bosses." He started with the floor nearest Wilbur, sweeping fragments into a pile with a push broom. "I'm not quite sure how. They probably wouldn't believe what really happened."

The newspaper flicked down. Wilbur met his gaze, the ghost of a smile on his face. He shifted his chair and lifted his feet, allowing Pierson to whisk the last remnants away.

"Thanks." He pushed the heap into a dustpan.

The newspaper went back up.

From the back room, Pierson scrounged a couple pieces of lumber he could use as a makeshift counter. Plans for a new deck, originally attached to the top board with a push pin, fluttered to the floor. There weren't enough pieces to complete the job, of course. But he'd gotten a reprieve from constant nagging when he'd announced that he'd started purchasing supplies a little at a time.

He sighed and picked the paper up. If he had actually completed the deck, instead of merely promising to build it year after year, then his ex-wife might still be *the* wife.

He lugged the boards out front and hoisted them high enough to protect the items on display. Rough, but it would do. A lesson he should have learned long ago.

Hanging his head in discouragement from tarrying so much, he cleaned the last of the glass from the display case, then stared at the now-useless deck plans.

The bell jingled as the door opened. In walked Angus, his chest puffed out and his head held high.

"I've managed to find an investor." He hooked a thumb into his front pocket. "Aye, I dare say, this is as good an agreement as you'll ever find. The management of the store remains completely in your hands and you have equal ownership. All you have to do is sign and write a check for three percent of the purchase price." With a small flourish, Angus placed a formal sales contract on top of the newly repaired counter. He tapped a sentence near the top, where a dollar amount, underlined and in bold print, practically jumped off the page.

Pierson let the plans for the new deck fall to the floor. "I've just been cleaned out in my divorce, and you expect me to put that much cash down?"

"Aye." Angus nodded, his tone nonchalant.

Pierson rubbed the back of his neck, willing away tension before it developed into a headache. If he signed a check for three percent of the purchase price, even though the percentage was low, it would take another fifteen years before he could save up enough for Costa Rica.

"I can't." Pierson pushed the contract back toward Angus. "I just can't."

Angus stared at him, mouth agape. "A deal like this doesn't come about but once in a lifetime. And the place will still be sold, one way or another."

"I know." Pierson swallowed hard. He could almost taste salt, imagining himself sipping margaritas on a Costa Rican beach.

Angus stared at Pierson, his clear blue eyes guileless, focused. He took a slow step back, leaving the contract on the countertop. "Look it over anyway. I'll come back to follow up with you at the end of the week."

The answer wouldn't change. But Pierson nodded. "Okay."

Angus veered before going out the door. "Good morning, Wilbur. Someday you'll have to tell me how you manage to get a daily print version of the newspaper. Everyone else I know reads the news online."

Silence, as expected, was the only response, before the door closed behind the Scotsman.

Pierson picked up the contract the next day, telling himself it was just for curiosity's sake Perusing the document, he conceded Angus was right. Even if he'd set the terms himself, they couldn't be more favorable to him without being unfair to any of the other parties.

His gaze lingered on the last name of the principal investor. Vernon. The name didn't stand out to him, particularly. Where had his old Scotsman buddy found such a willing, and generous, silent partner?

Still mulling things over, Pierson got up to stretch his legs and walk around The Olde Tobacco Bullion Shoppe. He'd held this job longer than any other in his life. He truly enjoyed it. Although the storefront was a simple one, its glass cases displayed an abundance of gold and silver jewelry. To be fair, turnover wasn't rapid—although most pieces exemplified high quality and good value, they were out of style. And even the finest diamond ring wouldn't fetch one-tenth its value once people saw it as a "used" ring instead of new.

He added other factors to his mental appraisal. The worn carpet in the store desperately needed a good cleaning. So did the inventory in the back room, especially the collections of random items with little intrinsic merit that had been stored for months, if not years. And the view outside of his window consisted of a parking lot and a busy highway, a far cry from the blue skies and ocean front vistas of his dream home in Costa Rica.

A familiar car eased into the closest customer spot.

The beauty was back again. Now a regular customer, she was going through her collection of silver coins, one small transaction at a time.

Pierson sighed as she came in the door. Somehow, he was feeling generous today. Maybe reading the terms of the sales contract put him in a benevolent mood. So he gave her twelve cans for her cats, today, instead of the customary six. "Here you go. Six kitties, twelve cans. They definitely won't have to share their dinner tonight."

Her soft brown eyes shone with gratitude. "They're getting big, so they eat more. Thank you so much!" She waved at Wilbur on her way out.

The newspaper dipped, ever so slightly, in response.

Pierson logged the new coin into inventory, then added "cans of tuna fish" to his shopping list. He snorted. Whenever the dark-haired music teacher showed up, he melted into a teddy bear, as gentle as her soft brown eyes. He wasn't too keen on it becoming a new norm for him. He was the last of the knuckle-dragging Cro-Magnons, after all. Wasn't he?

A bedraggled older man, stooped and slightly below medium height, walked in, eyes downcast. He wore faded blue jeans, a ball cap emblazoned with a bald eagle, and a T-shirt with the reverse outline of a U.S. flag.

Pierson straightened his shoulders. He recognized the motif.

Army.

Although he was a former marine, he knew the legend, a favorite for members of the U.S. Army men. The reversed flag duplicated the way it would look whenever the flag bearer led the way during a charge. The fact that few, if any, infantrymen still participated in such charges was irrelevant.

The customer took off his ball cap and shuffled to the counter. He favored his right leg slightly, wincing with each step, although Pierson guessed he masked most of the pain under a tough, workingman exterior.

He schooled his own expression to neutral. A fellow warrior would not welcome sympathy.

The man placed a golden chain on the counter.

Pierson's heart sank. Even without touching it, he could tell it was nothing but metallic junk.

Sometimes, it was preferable to let the customers see for themselves rather than just take his word for it when there was bad news. So he opened the drawer with his appraisal tools and pulled out a magnet.

With a slithering sound, the chain leapt toward the magnet and bunched up along the axis.

Pierson shook his head slowly and handed the chain back.

"I'll be a sunnova..." The man took a deep breath. "At least I know, right?" He slid the worthless piece into his pocket.

A hollow spot in the pit of Pierson's gut lurched. "We can always do this again sometime. You never know what might be real gold."

The old man slumped. "Grandson's birthday's this weekend. But I've been spending so much money on medical bills, I'm having trouble making ends meet."

Pierson scrutinized him, looking for telltale inconsistencies. Customers of all types walked into his store. Over the years, he'd developed a knack for being able to tell when one was sincere or not. But, there was always that occasional one—like McFarrell—who could hide their duplicity. Was this man on the level? Did he dare find out?

He cleared his throat. "Vietnam?"

"Two tours."

"Wait here." Pierson headed to the back of the store and returned with the one-ounce silver Liberty Bell coin that McFarrell had dropped.

He placed it on the counter. "On the house." It was paid for, after all. He didn't expect the state senator would come back any time soon. And he'd wager his next paycheck that the Army vet would see to it that his grandson valued the patriotic coin properly. "As a thank you for your service."

The old man's eyes shone. His hand trembled when he picked up the coin. He walked a little straighter as he limped toward the exit, donning his bald-eagle ball cap along the way.

Wilbur's newspaper rattled.

The man sketched a brief salute, acknowledging the other veteran. "Good afternoon."

Naturally, silence filled the room until the jingle of the bell above the door announced the old man's departure.

The newspaper rattled again.

Pierson let out a heavy sigh. Running a charity was certainly not the soundest of business practices. But, God help him, he couldn't resist.

He reached for the contract to buy the store, which still sat on top of his desk, and a ballpoint pen. He still didn't know the main buyer. Relying on Angus's reassurances alone meant a real leap of faith.

Ink glided over the page.

"There." He clicked the pen and retracted the point, then placed it carefully on the counter. "I've signed it."

"Good!" Wilbur stood. His voice, soft spoken yet emphatic, reverberated in the quiet room. He placed his newspaper on the nearest chair and promptly walked out the door.

Pierson stared through the storefront window as the outline of Wilbur's tall form receded in the distance. In all of the years he had worked at the store, that was the first time Pierson had ever heard Wilbur speak.

He picked up the contract and turned to the last page. He and Angus were co-owners, along with the principal purchaser, whose name was George W. Vernon.

Could it be?

But of course it was. It had to be. After all, a lot of people went by their middle names. Who else but Wilbur would be willing to sign an agreement on such favorable terms?

Pierson brushed a fingertip over the contract where his "silent" partner's name was inscribed and chuckled lightly.

Yes, Costa Rica was far off in the distance. Maybe he'd never get there. But, somehow, it no longer mattered. And for the first time in many years, Pierson felt calm and content, at home in the Olde Tobacco Bullion Shoppe.

ARTIST'S REVENGE

By Bob Rich

Despite physical limitations, Wyn is a talented artist, driven by his passion for painting. In this realistic fiction, he navigates contrasting reactions of two young women he meets at the beach.

Bob Rich is an Australian storyteller, with nineteen published books. Six of them and over forty short stories have won awards.

He's retired five times from five different occupations, but is still going strong as a professional grandfather. Everything he does is working toward a survivable future—and one worth surviving in—for all his grandchildren.

He carries on much of this work at his blog, *Bobbing Around,* at bobrich18.wordpress.com.

He discovered he was a Buddhist at twenty-three years of age, when a Christian minister of religion told him. He spent a day in the library to check this claim. To his surprise, he found his philosophy set out in beautiful words by the Buddha. He is not fussed by death, having done it all too many times.

Artist's Revenge

YOUNG WOMEN ARE a sweet agony, a toyshop I'll never enter. I'm a moth, forever singeing the wings of my soul, stupidly circling toward destruction.

Courting ridicule, courting rejection, I instruct my prison on wheels to advance across the Esplanade, stopping against the wrought iron railing.

And there is my other love, the one that gives me nothing but joy. Well out, the rollers rise, turn from azure to turquoise, relentlessly rush at the shore until their front is an impossible incline, and their tops boil with foam, until they break and fall with a roar of thunder. The concrete under my wheels vibrates with the shock of their ever-repeated assault. Our house faces the most beautiful beach in all of Australia.

A thousand times have I seen the beach in all its moods, and always it is different. A dozen times have I tried to capture the grandeur in my paintings. Others praise my work, even with the ultimate praise of a purchase, though they know nothing of the twisted wreck I am. To me, my attempts are ever short of the real: the living sea meeting the immovable shore.

The beach is an expanse of gold sprinkled with people. Wherever my eyes roam, they light upon rounded breasts seeking to escape skimpy restraints, flaring hips and flashing legs, hair of gold and chestnut and anthracite blown by the breath of the sea.

Torture.

Someone casts a shadow. A head intrudes between me and the sun. "Disgusting," a cold female voice says. "They should lock things like that away."

"Don't be unkind." This is from a higher voice, perhaps even younger. "He can hear you."

A tinkling laugh, a musical sound of amusement that chainsaws into my heart. "Who says he can even hear? Or if he can, would he understand? That thing?"

I should pretend. I should be the idiot of her supposition. I should sit, mute and immobile and invisibly bleeding, and wait for them to move on before returning to my lair. But my lips click the control and my tongue turns the little ball. My chair spins on the spot, and I face them.

Long, shapely, suntanned legs end at tomato-red panties so brief they barely cover her secret spaces.

An expanse of smooth brown abdomen stretches to luscious red-clothed swellings above, the nipples outlined against the material. Still higher, hair of deep gold, lighter at the tips, frames a heart-shaped face. The cruel, scornful eyes are blue, blue, bluer than the sea. A little, pert nose, a grimace of distaste on the full lips I'll never kiss.

Beyond, long, straight hair of burnished bronze partly hides a plain face, covered with freckles. Her eyes, same color as her hair, look through thick, blue-rimmed glasses. She wears a shapeless white T-shirt and a pair of shorts, but even these don't hide the chubbiness of her torso. There is no cruelty here, but I see worse: pity.

Language is a snail. Better than a picture, better than a photograph, all this I've seen in an instant, and it will be with me for all of my life. Fate has imposed the cruelty of cerebral palsy but was kind with eidetic imagery—whenever I choose, one glance gives me a record I can see at will, and later examine in the minutest detail. This is my liberation, my sanity, my ecstasy, the tool of my work.

During that instant, I see the red-haired girl start forward. She is past her friend, then between her and me, and she bends. The salty breeze strokes my face with the tips of her hair, then her lips touch my cheek. "Please forgive her," she says, her breath on my skin, then she is past, she is gone, and the two of them walk down to the beach, down the stairs, that impassable barrier to wheels.

Not pity but compassion. I can accept compassion, which is the hand of one sufferer held out to another.

That night, and for many nights after, my futile dreams will be about red hair and a freckled face.

I turn my chair to face the beach once more, to track their progress across the sand. The red-haired girl turns, her glasses flashing the sun into my eyes, and she raises a hand in farewell.

When their shapes have dissolved into the distance, into the crowd, I work my little control wheel, telling my chair to return home. I trundle up the driveway, up the ramp, and bump through the back door.

I pass Harker, who is helping himself to some milk. "G'day, Wyn," he says, smiling. Harker, two years younger, my brother, my mate, my liberator. He chose his occupation, his life's work, so he could design electronic wonders for my use: the chair, the bed, the six devices that together allow me to paint.

I spit out the control. The chair stops. "I'd like to start a new painting," I tell him. Of all the people in the world, only two understand my words: Harker and Mother.

He carries his glass and walks beside me to my room. From here, the beach is a distant background through the eastern window that's half a wall. My wonderful bed is against the west wall, under the ceiling rails of the lifting machine, which is now parked over the bath.

He takes the current, quarter-finished painting off the easel. It is the size of four A4 sheets, the top left-hand quadrant complete. One day, if ever I return to it, it will be a yellow rose with bright sunlight caught in little droplets of water.

Harker leans the board against the wall and looks at me with a question.

"Eight by four," I say, and he whistles in surprise. I have just asked him to set up several months of work.

While he is fetching a board of suitable size, and adjusting the easel, and tacking up sheets of blank paper, I stop the chair at my workstation, facing the screen. This screen is worth more than the house.

The computer control sits on its holder, which is a flexible stalk. I spit out the chair control, and after a few attempts "swallow the mouse," an old family joke.

And for hours at a time, every day, I work on the two girls. Each of thirty-two sheets is eight frames, and a frame might take me an hour, or a day.

I look at the easel with its numbered pages, and I can see projected onto it the painting as it will be. I choose a page, and a segment of it the size of a business card. I start a blank frame, which is a white sheet on the screen magnified ten times. Click, click, click, I use the marvelous tools of my graphics program to create electronic brush strokes that fill the screen with living color. Three hours pass as, pixel by pixel, I create the left lens of the glasses, half a minute to modify a mirror image for the right.

When the eight frames of a page are done, I activate the printer, Harker's printer that uses acrylic paints. When all the layers are dry, Mother or Harker glues the sheet carefully into place, and I can move onto another tile of my mosaic.

I am resting. Through the window, I admire the winter storm lashing the sea into fury, so the house shakes in sympathy with the pounding surf. Behind me, on the easel, the painting is all but complete. Only two blank pages remain, both of them mostly background.

Headlights stabbing through the rain, wipers working hard, a white Mercedes eases to a stop before our house. A blue umbrella pokes its tip above the driver's door, on the far side, then advances with quick little bumps around the front. I can now see it in full, providing inadequate shelter for Ingrid, who is wearing a matching blue raincoat. She scurries toward the front door and passes out of my sight.

Ingrid is my agent. She is a middle-aged fount of enthusiasm and energy, encouragement and advice, the buffer between the world of art and the secret of my accursed body.

I turn my chair and wait. The door opens, and Mother leads Ingrid into the room. She has shed her raincoat, but her cream-colored slacks are wet below the knees. She is rubbing obviously cold hands together, her face bearing a friendly smile. "Been a while, Wyn," she says. I watch her face as the painting captures her attention. She stops. Even her hands stop their rubbing. She takes a deep breath.

"Cruelty and compassion," she says at last. "It's the best you've ever done."

The painting shows heads only, both in three-quarter profile. The two girls face away from each other. On the left is the blonde. I have painted her beautiful, even more beautiful than in real life, but as you look at her lovely face, it becomes ugly: cold, rejecting, crippled within as it is perfect outside.

The redhead on the right is the opposite. At first, your eyes slide over her plain, ordinary visage and are instead captured by the other. But when you return, you see Goodness, and Love, the universal Mother though she is young; I have painted her younger than she is.

"Wyn, I love you," Ingrid says. She hurries to me, and bends to give my cheek a kiss. I breathe in her perfume. She straightens but strokes my hair with a delicate hand. "Finish it, and we'll enter it in the Archibald."

The Archibald Prize is an annual event. Artists from all around Australia submit portraits, mostly of the famous, but the identity of the model doesn't matter. It is a painting competition, not a parade of people.

Of course, I won't win, but I'm happy to be in it.

More months have passed. I have completed two more paintings, and last week Mother took me on an outing to the bush. I have absorbed the spring awakening of the Australian landscape. Oh, it's not as showy as that of other lands, its beauty is subtle. Giant, gnarled gumtrees turn red at the tips with new growth, and one of them is taking shape on the canvas of my computer.

Concentrating, I am barely aware of the phone ringing in another room, in another reality. But then Mother's little shriek pulls me back into the world. Is something wrong?

She rushes in. "Wyn, love, that was Ingrid. You're shortlisted for the Archibald!"

I wish they hadn't told me. I wish they'd kept it a secret. Now I have hope. I lose sleep and can't concentrate on my work. If I could, I would chew my fingernails, the way Harker does when he is worried. Time now becomes a cripple like me, and walks in glue.

Weeks pass. I finish my tree from a sense of duty, but then lack inspiration for a new project. Harker sets up the ancient yellow rose to give me something to do.

At last, Ingrid lets us know. No, I didn't win, not even a minor placing, of course not. But, a few weeks later, an official invitation arrives in the mail, forwarded through by Ingrid. The envelope also holds a newspaper clipping—a review in the *Sydney Morning Herald* of "the compelling, intriguing, vibrant masterpiece titled 'Cruelty and Compassion' by mystery artist Wynstanley Thompson."

And so I lose more sleep. Will I? Won't I? But eventually I make a momentous decision. For the first time ever, I'll risk being seen by my public.

Travel is a chore, but at long last we are there. An elegant crowd swirls around the exhibits. Harker makes way for my chair, while Ingrid and Mother flank me as I head for the winner.

I can see why it won. It is a wonderful portrait, in a way non-representational, full of deliberate distortions that bring the well-known personality to life. I'll study this painting at home within the gallery of my mind, and learn from it.

The paintings are arranged in order of merit, and to my surprise, my girls are in fifth place. "Excellent, for a first try," Ingrid tells me.

People jostle each other. My chair is a reef in the tide as I move to the sixth painting. Over the constant hubbub of the crowd, I hear a shriek, "That's me!"

I can't help it. I spin my chair.

It is the blonde, though of course wearing a stylish dress and sparkling jewelry. She holds the hand of a large older man in a dark suit. Her eyes are upon her likeness, at first with pride, and then, as she looks, her face freezes over.

She must feel my gaze upon her, for she turns. Naked swords, our eyes cross. "Oh. The freak," she says. Then she spins away and jerks on her escort's hand. They disappear in the crowd.

Revenge is sweet, at first. For days, I see the dismay upon her face, the hurt I inflicted by forcing self-knowledge upon her. But then doubt comes, for am I not as bad? Perhaps she is a helpless victim of the handicap of her emotions, as I am a helpless victim of the handicap of my body.

One morning, I sit looking out my window at the empty weekday beach, seagulls wheeling over surf, when the phone rings. And then, Mother calls, "Wyn, it's for you, love!"

I trundle over. Mother has activated the loudspeaker, and Ingrid says, "Wyn, darling, a young woman has tracked me down. She says she met you once, and has often thought of you since, and wants to meet you again. Her name is Cybil Martin."

My heart dances a mad pitter-patter, and my voice is slurred, worse than ever, as I ask a question. Mother translates, "Ingrid, what's the color of her hair?"

Ingrid laughs in surprise. "I haven't met her, just talked with her on the phone. I can ask."

But I know the answer. It is the color of burnished bronze.

TEACHING YOUNG KIDS

By Sunayna Pal

Teaching is not for the faint of heart, but in this fictional piece, teaching small kids is an even greater feat. However, when the assignment is accepted, the joy of impacting young minds is the reward.

Sunayna Pal's poetry graces the pages of numerous international journals, anthologies, museums, poetry festivals, textbooks, and libraries, resonating with readers worldwide.

Her debut book, *Refugees in Their Own Country* (B&W Fountain), vividly narrates the Partition of India through evocative verse and illustrations, while her second book, *Please Go to the Park* (Bottlecap Press), is an invitation to embark on a journey of self-discovery. As the Director of The Poetry Academy, Sunayna nurtures a deep appreciation for poetry in others. She is dedicated to Heartfulness meditation.

Residing in Maryland with her family, Sunayna invites readers to explore her work and journey at *sunaynapal.com*.

"WHERE'S THE CALCI?" I asked the group of five other teachers who sat on the floor of the classroom. I stood near one of the corners, so I tried a little louder. "Anyone listening? I need the calculator to do accounts."

But the other teachers were engrossed in their work. We volunteered at a non-profit organization, Touching Lives, which we referred to as "the shelter." We taught kids from families that had left their homes in rural India and come to Mumbai in search of better lives. Many of these kids who came to the shelter were over ten years of age. Because they didn't know basic English, they couldn't learn the remaining subjects. In just a few years, they needed to pass their state exams and go to college. I taught this vulnerable group of students Math.

From my corner of the artwork-covered room, I spotted my student Abdul using my calci. His class was over, but he had stayed back with a few others to finish homework. I sighed, closed my eyes, and added the numbers in my mind.

After I opened my eyes, I noticed a girl sitting near the door with her school bag on her shoulder. At a guess, she was barely five or six years old. Her class must have ended at least an hour ago, but she had to wait for her elder sister to finish lessons before they could go home.

She smiled at me.

I smiled back. I am fond of little kids, but I prefer teaching older students. Although I had volunteered at the shelter for over six months, I had never mentioned this to anyone. I didn't need to, because three of my colleagues had already withdrawn from teaching the older ones. I think the teenagers' attitudes annoyed them, or maybe they required more patience so they focused on the youngsters.

I, on the other hand, found it difficult to teach these single-digit-aged kids and their erratic loads of questions. Sometimes I think they add "Why" at the end and start of everything they say, even when they don't need any explanations. I am the eldest cousin in my generation, with over a dozen inquisitive relatives after me. I can surely say that I have dealt with enough aggravating questions for a lifetime.

The small girl crawled up to me and broke my train of thought.

I shouldn't have smiled back.

"Didi," she called, in a sing-song fashion.

I cringed a little. Now the questions would begin.

"What are you doing, Didi?" Her purple floral frock was a size too small. Threads peeked out on all the seams.

I took a deep breath. "Finishing accounts."

She peered at the ledger. "Why? What are accounts?"

I tried to simplify the concept. "I'm trying to equal the money. Our expenses should balance the donations we get."

"How do you know what numbers to write?"

"I added them in my head."

"Why? Can you add big numbers by closing your eyes?"

I ignored the why. "Yes. Not very big ones."

"Why is learning math always useful, Didi?"

There it was again. "Because numbers are everywhere. Everyone uses them. Tailors, chefs, engineers, teachers, and . . ."

Before I could think of more examples, her elder sister called. "Come, Chutki."

Chutki promptly got up and followed her sister out of the room. I let go of the breath I wasn't aware of holding.

Checking my work, I realized I had to re-add the digits column. I closed my eyes, but felt a tap on my shoulder. I counted to three before I turned around.

The manager, Sonia, gazed at me with eyes wider than normal and a big grin on her face.

I clenched my pencil. Why was she smiling like this?

She drew a circle with her index finger. "I overheard this sweet conversation. Do you think you could teach basic mathematics to the younger kids as well?"

I stared at her.

"The current teacher isn't able to reach them." She circled her fingers again. "You not only connected with Chutki but also seemed to have made her interested in this problematic subject." A grin flashed across her face. "No pun intended."

She laughed.

I didn't.

"I think this was wonderful. I know you might have a lot on your plate already. I'll put an ad in online groups for a new teacher. But in the meantime, do you think you could handle the class for a few days?" Sonia asks.

"Wh—" I tried to find my way out without using the word I hated to hear from the little ones. "I mean . . . will changing so many teachers be good for the kids? Let the old one continue till the new one joins."

"She could, but you know things are not working out with her."

I gulped.

She shrugged. "Also, even after we find a new teacher, he or she will have to be trained. Kids might be better off with you, and then you can train the new teacher."

"Okay, let me think about it."

"Yes, absolutely." She beamed, as if I'd already agreed.

The next day, Sonia sat outside the entrance of the shelter. Was she waiting for me? I couldn't tell, but just like yesterday, her eyes were wider than usual, full of questions—or maybe only one question. *Have you made your decision already*? As I removed my shoes and passed her to go inside, she grinned but said nothing.

When I went inside to get coffee, she joined me there, too. Was she going to follow me around?

I realized that I had two options. Tell her the truth—that I didn't like teaching the younger one—s or . . . Oh God! I couldn't even imagine the other one, but it was the right thing to do. I could teach for some time and decided to tell her. After a sip of coffee, I cleared my throat. "So, I was thinking . . ."

"Yes?" She rubbed her hands together.

"Yes, well I could teach for sometim—"

She didn't let me finish. "Oh! Thank you. You are the best. Can we start tomorrow? I'll ask the old teacher to train you today after the class."

I coughed, gasping for air. "Tomo— *Tomorrow* tomorrow?"

"Of course."

"I thought I'd have at least a month."

"You will be fine." She touched my arm. "Continue the way you did with Chutki."

Without another word, she left me with my coffee, and we didn't cross paths the rest of the day.

As I lay in bed that night, I considered calling in sick. But it wasn't a permanent solution. I wiped the sweat from my forehead and thought of ways of saying no.

One good thing was that Sonia and the others didn't know that I disliked young kids. What would they think about me if they found out?

Another good thing was that it was temporary. But an hour with them?

Actually . . . just an hour, thrice a week.

I considered my first day at the shelter, six months back. I hadn't been able to sleep the previous night. I knew if I wanted to make a difference in society, I had to do something practical about it. I was so nervous entering the shelter that I sat by the wall for support. But the day had gone well. I still remember the elation I had felt as I walked back home.

This was the same. I knew I had to find a way to teach these young minds tomorrow. I *could* do it. And with this determination, I finally fell asleep.

The next evening, I entered the part of the shelter where the young kids had classes for the first time. It was so colorful! Cleverly decorated, with animal pictures cut out from the newspaper and drawings of beautiful pink and purple flowers stuck on top of the peeling beige paint.

I walked into the classroom with a strong will, but my body didn't cooperate. My hands kept trembling. I wiped my forehead with my handkerchief

Five kids—four girls and one boy—between five and six years of age sat on the floor, legs crossed. Five thin bodies sitting squeezed together as if for protection.

Chutki, the girl who started it all, sat in the front wearing a green dress that seemed to be ripping at the seams. She looked nervous.

It somehow relaxed me, knowing I wasn't the only one.

In fact, all of them had frown lines. One girl nibbled the nail of her little finger. Two students stared at my feet, and one girl, who wore faded clothes, looked at the board, not me.

Why are kids—or adults—so scared of numbers? I have always found Math to be the easiest subject, because two plus two will always be four. Personally, once the basics are learned, everything else is just as simple.

At that moment, I knew what to do. I had to somehow remove this fear they felt.

Following Sonia's advice, and the cue from my conversation with Chutki, I posed a question. "Where do you all think we use math?

"Sch—school?" One of the girls, still staring at my feet, stammered her reply.

"Yes! Good job! Where else?" I nodded at Chutki. Perhaps she remembered the discussion from the other day. "Chutki, where have you seen numbers?"

Chutki smiled, but her eyes were blank.

One of the girls waved her hand. "I saw some on the knob on the fan."

"Good observation. Yes, the fan is slow when it is on 1 and super-fast like a helicopter when it is on 5."

They giggled.

"So, numbers indicate the speed?"

"Yes, Didi." The students answered simultaneously.

"Knowing numbers is important." I took a deep breath. "Where else have you seen it?"

"My dad is a tailor," murmured the only boy in the group.

"Oh, wonderful. And?"

"He uses numbers to measure clothes."

"Very good." I clapped. "Can you think of any other job where numbers are used?"

The child in the faded clothes sat up. "My neighbor is a carpenter. He has a measuring tape."

"Yes, good. A measuring tape has numbers."

"Pilots use numbers?" The boy guessed.

Chutki nodded her agreement. "Yes, a plane must be filled with numbers." She looked at me. "Didi, even painters, engineers, bakers—all need numbers. *Haina*?"

"Perfect. Yes! Yes, they do."

"But why, Didi?"

"To measure everything. Numbers are everywhere. You cannot work without them." I finally knew the answer to a Why question. "Have you been to a grocery shop?"

They nodded but said nothing.

"Yes! Good! Have you seen numbers there?"

The girl who had been biting her nails clapped her hands with excitement. "Money is numbers?"

"Yes, it is. Very good."

She beamed.

An idea came to me. "Okay, suppose the shopkeeper says that the total bill is eight rupees. If your mom gives him a ten rupees note, how much should the shopkeeper give back?"

Chutki leaned in and opened her mouth, but nothing came out. It looked as if she knew the answer but was afraid to say it aloud.

I prompted her gently. "Chutki, do you know how much the shopkeeper should return?"

"Two?" she asked meekly.

"Awesome. How did you count?"

She showed me ten fingers, then took away eight.

Palms to my cheeks in fake surprise, I leaned in. "You guys know sutbraction." I covered my mouth and giggled. "I mean *subtraction*."

They giggled in return.

I settled into my seat. "I don't believe this. Why do you need me? Let me give you more questions."

They giggled so loudly that Sonia peeked inside, smiled at me, and gave a small wave when she left.

As I gave the kids more problems, I realized that all five of them knew the basics. I only needed to take the fear away from them and help them to become aware of their already present skills.

Also, I wasn't trembling anymore.

Their eyes didn't leave the board while I quizzed them on single-digit and double-digit addition and subtraction. Chalk powder flew through the air as I tested all of them together and then individually. They all got it.

They all really got it.

I saw them all count on their fingers, and before I knew it, the class was over.

I had never felt happier. I had made them giggle. I had taught them. This felt beyond awesome. Even better than my first day at the shelter.

Maybe it was just me, but it seemed there was extra light in the room that day when they packed their bags and hung them on their shoulders. None of them actually asked any weird questions. I felt sure I could teach them for a few days, at least.

As I bid them goodbye, I couldn't stop grinning. I sat on the floor mat, eager to prepare the paperwork for the next day.

In the nearby room, Sonia asked Chutki, "How was the math class?"

"Sonia Didi, I'll pass my exams."

"What do you mean?"

"I was afraid I'd fail. Now, I think I'll pass."

"That's awesome." Sonia's voice held enthusiasm.

"Will Didi continue to teach us?"

"Hmm! Let's see. Will you be waiting for your sister again?"

"Maybe."

And in less than a minute, Sonia walked into the room with an enormous smile and the widest eyes I had ever seen. "So, I was thinking . . ."

My grin didn't disappear as I said, "The answer is yes. I will continue to teach them."

THE BROTHER

By Daniel Warner

Kyle isn't happy his father decided to sell off North Fork Ranch without consulting him, but he's outraged to learn the profits will go to his brother. In this contemporary fiction, two brothers spar over an inheritance that likely will destroy what's left of their family.

Daniel Warner's debut novel, *The Wolf and the Lamb*, was named a semi-finalist in the prestigious ACFW Genesis contest. He was honored to be selected as a member of Jenkins' inaugural Mastermind Inner Circle group.

Warner's Burning Bush blogs, designed to equip men with biblical knowledge and leadership skills, provide interesting 15-minute Bible studies that model a simple 4-step process for analyzing Scripture.

Daniel lives in Florida with his wife of fifteen years and his dog Kipling. He retired after twenty-five years in the corporate world, filling roles from software engineer to manager of large development teams. Warner leads a team of deacons in his local church and facilitates an adult Sunday School class. Find the Burning Bush blogs and more from Daniel at *danielpwarner.com*.

The Brother

THE MOMENT I entered the conference room I saw my ex sitting next to my brother. Her hand lingered on his arm.

I stopped cold. "What's she doing here?"

Pops shifted his eyes down. "Have a seat, Son. And take off your hat."

I remained standing. "Nice dress, Charlotte. Could it be more revealing?"

"Good to see you too." She flashed me a saccharine smile.

"You and her a thing now?" I plopped across from my brother, ignoring the manilla file on the table. "I'll ask again—why is she here?"

"It's all there in front of you." Tripp didn't meet my stare.

I slid the folder forward, clearing room for my elbows. "Been a long day. Don't feel like reading paperwork. What's with the sudden meeting, Pops?"

He finally glanced up. His eyes looked dark, like he hadn't slept in days. "We've decided to sell off North Fork."

I started to laugh, then realized they were serious. "We? Who's *we*? I wasn't consulted."

"He doesn't need to consult you, Kyle," my brother said. "It's not your ranch."

"Tripp, I know it's not my–but that's not the point. He said *we* decided."

"Yeah," Charlotte said. "Your father and Tripp."

"Pops, I don't get it." I leaned in. "North Fork is just becoming profitable. Our customers love the new quarters–and where we gonna launch our rafts from?"

Tripp shrugged. "Package deal. We sold off the white-water business too."

"Okay." I rubbed my forehead. "That must have fetched a good price. What're we doing with the money?"

Pops glanced at Tripp. "This is your rodeo. You explain it to him."

"Uh . . ." My brother tapped the file folder.

"It's Tripp's money." Charlotte tilted her head in challenge. "Doesn't involve you anymore, Kyle."

My face started to burn. "What are you talking about? Tripp, please tell me you have a plan."

He cleared his throat. "We've got some investors."

Charlotte beamed. "A consortium."

"Right," Tripp said. "A consortium of real estate investors. Charlotte and I are launching a startup."

"With Pop's money?"

"What don't you get?" Charlotte's eyes flashed. "It's Tripp's money."

I glared at her. "What don't *you* get? The money came from selling off North Fork."

"It's Tripp's inheritance. He's just taking it early. While he's young." She squeezed his hand. "So he can make something of himself."

Flabbergasted, I leaned back in my chair. My mouth moved, but no words came out. I swiveled and glared at Pop's attorney, sitting next to my father. "Zak, how could you let them talk him into this?"

Pops raised his hand before Zak could respond. "It's my ranch, Son. Decision is made. Wish your brother luck in his endeavors. We made South Fork work on its own before and we'll do it again."

"Sure, Pops, I'm with you. But wish him luck? How can he get his inheritance while you're still alive? It's like he's wishing you dead already!"

Tripp shot me a dirty look. "That's enough, Kyle! Dad made this decision on his own, and Zak got us a great price. They both understand the opportunity sitting in front of me."

Zak fiddled with the papers, seemingly unwilling to meet my stare. I shifted my scowl Charlotte's way. "Real estate? Is this the same timeshare scheme your cousin pitched us?"

"It's not a timeshare," Tripp said. "These are commercial properties that each investor owns a portion of."

I snorted. "Like I said, a timeshare."

"They aren't travel resorts! They—"

"Forget him, Baby." Charlotte nestled even tighter against my brother. "He never understood the business plan. He's just jealous he didn't think of this funding model."

I slammed my fist on the table. "Funding model! This ain't no funding model! This is destroying half of what Pops and I worked our whole lives to build! And you're just taking the money? At the least, your father should be one of your investors! This is robbery!"

Pops stepped around the table during my rant and snaked an arm around my shoulder. "The consortium members weren't gonna dilute their shares. Tripp's entitled to his inheritance. I'd do the same thing for you, if you asked."

"I wouldn't ask! This is an outrage!"

Shaking off Pops's arm, I grabbed the folder and slung it at my brother. I stomped out the door as papers flew everywhere.

Eighteen months later

The chirping phone startled me. I glanced at the glowing screen. I didn't recognize the number, but it was two in the morning. And Pops was in the hospital. So I answered.

"Kyle? This is Charlotte. I'm sorry to wake you."

"You didn't wake me. Just got back from the gas station. My wife is pregnant."

"That's great. Congrats."

Alicia propped herself up on her pillow. "Is that Charlotte?"

I nodded and tilted the device so she could hear too. "Why are you calling me, Charlotte? Tripp in some kinda trouble?"

"He's in jail, Kyle. And I might be next."

I paused to let the news sink in. The only part that surprised me was how quickly the fall had happened. "What do you expect me to do about it?"

"He's still your brother."

"No he isn't."

"Kyle—"

"I'm surprised you didn't call Pops."

She sighed. "We tried, but Zak answered. He said your father will be fine, so I don't understand why he wouldn't let us talk to him."

"He's recovering from a heart attack! The doctor said—"

"That's why I'm calling you."

"Forget it, Charlotte, I'm not able to help you."

"Then I'll keep trying to reach your father."

"You can't do that. If he finds out Tripp's in jail, the stress will kill him. Literally."

"Then *you* need to do something, Kyle. Because I'm not going to jail with Tripp."

Alicia touched my arm. "Kyle, you should help. He *is* your blood. And your father needs to be kept out of this. Our boy will need his grandfather."

"Oh, he'll have his grandfather," I said, my frustration mounting.

"Kyle," Charlotte said. "I'm not playing."

I just wanted out of this conversation. "How'd he end up in jail? Scratch that, I don't care. What are you asking for, anyway?"

"Eleven thousand dollars."

"Eleven thousand! What for?"

"Ten thousand for Tripp's bail. The rest to keep me out."

"How's a thousand dollars gonna keep you out? You gonna bribe someone?"

"The lady said she wouldn't press charges if I paid her back."

"What lady? Never mind, I don't want to know. But I don't see how I can raise that kind of money."

"Okay, I'll try your father again."

"You're sick!"

"We can swing it, Hon," Alicia said. "Just tell this psychopath never to contact my husband again."

I shook my head. "No way. We're not touching our emergency fund."

"I can hear you two talking," Charlotte said. "If this doesn't classify as an emergency, I don't know what does. You need to wire me the money first thing in the morning. And since you're calling me a psychopath, make it twelve grand. That way I have some get-away money."

How had I ever let that woman get her claws into me? And how had I ever let this happen to Tripp? We had been so close once. Why hadn't I seen it coming?

I felt like flinging the phone against the wall. But Alicia's grip tightened around my arm. Strong, for a pregnant woman. "Just get this over with," she whispered.

I breathed out.

"Okay, Charlotte, two conditions. One, you don't tell Tripp where you got the money. Two, I never hear from either of you again. And don't you *ever* try to contact Pops."

"That's three conditions, but no problem. Soon as I bail out Tripp, I'm gone. Never expected him to be such a loser."

Twelve months later

Our exhausted group rode out of the backcountry before sunset. I had promised an adventurous week of fishing in the mountains, but the greenhorns hadn't bargained on the rough weather and terrain. Somehow, after several hours ride into the wilderness, they even seemed to find the lack of private bathrooms surprising. I had worked harder than usual to help them catch an abundance of trout, set up and tear down the tents, and pack out their waste. Even so, the tip was low and their complaints amongst themselves too audible for my liking.

Dusty and irritable, I led the horses into the corral and stripped them down. South Fork was oddly quiet. Where were all the hired hands? All I wanted was to get home to Alicia and the baby, but I had responsibilities.

Finally, Jethro emerged from the mess tent. I was hoping he'd be carrying a bowl of stew, but no such luck.

"Kyle, let me take care of the horses. Why ain't you at your father's house?"

"Just got back. Why would I go to Pops's? I only wanna go home."

"Didn't you check your phone? He's throwing a big party. Everyone's supposed to go. Only a bare-bones staff supposed to stay behind. That means me, I guess."

"Been in the mountains. No use taking my phone back there. Why's he throwing a party?"

Jethro looked uncomfortable. "I don't know. But you better be gittin' up there."

Twenty minutes later, I drove through the gates of Pops's estate. Pickups and horses were everywhere. The aroma of a roasting pig wafted through my cracked windows. Music blared from inside the house. Was that a D.J.?

I parked around the side and called Alicia a second time. "I'm at his house. You still don't know what this is about? Looks nuts."

"No, Hon. Can't seem to reach anyone. They must all be inside. Why don't you go find out?"

"I smell like fish. And other stuff. And I look worse than I smell. Wouldn't be respectful."

She snorted. "Pops don't care 'bout that. Who do you need to impress, anyway?"

"I'll call you back."

I stepped out and leaned against the 4x4. Unease filled my soul. I couldn't remember the last time Pops had thrown a bash like this.

I convinced myself I was too tired to go in. Didn't want to get stuck talking to a bunch of people about a disastrous guide trip into the mountains. I started to reach for my truck's door handle when I noticed Pops's attorney, Zak, rushing my way.

"Kyle! So glad you made it! Corbin's been asking about you. You look hungry."

"Pops inside?"

"Yes! Come on in, enjoy the food. The celebration has just begun!"

"Zak, I ain't up to it. I smell terrible, and I'm exhausted. What's this all about, anyway?"

"You don't know? Why don't you head inside. Corbin wanted to surprise you."

I was starting to figure it out, and I didn't like what my brain was telling me. "If Pops wants to tell me something, why doesn't he come out and tell me himself?"

"Your father—"

"It's Tripp, isn't it?"

Zak's eyes flickered, and I knew I was right. "Just go in and talk to him. Let him explain."

I crossed my arms. "No way. I'll give him five minutes, and then I'm outta here."

Clearly flustered, Zak hurried into the house.

Less than a minute later, Pops burst through the door and ran to me, his face flushed. "Kyle, I'm glad you're here. I didn't want to text you the truth. Figured you wouldn't show up."

"You got that right."

"Please come in and be civil. I beg of you, do it for me. Your brother—"

"My what?"

"Tripp wants—"

I stood my ground. "Did you know that I bailed him out of jail last year when you were in the hospital?"

"That was you? I'm grateful—"

"I did it for you, Pops. I've always obeyed you and served you faithfully. And this is how you repay me? You throw *Tripp* a welcome-back party. Like nothing ever happened! When did you ever throw one for me? The most I ever got was a birthday cookout with a few relatives."

"Obeyed? Served me? You think that's what I want out of you?" Pops reached for my face. "I love you, Kyle."

I flinched. "This son of yours has squandered away your property with prostitutes and thieves. He comes home and you roast a boar in his honor!"

"Kyle, my son," Pops said softly. "You're always with me, and everything I have is yours. But we must celebrate, because this brother of yours was dead and is alive again. He was lost and now is found."

"I'm going home to *my* family."

The next morning

I woke to find Alicia holding the baby in one arm and her Bible in the other. I yawned. "What time is it?"

"You were exhausted and didn't hear him cry," she said. "I let you sleep in."

"Why you reading that?"

"Kyle, I miss church. How long has it been?"

I shrugged. "Babe, you know how hard I'm working at South Fork. The weekends I don't guide, I need my rest."

"I was reading this passage from Luke."

"Why?"

"What you were telling me about Tripp. And Pops. Reminded me of the prodigal son parable, so I wanted to read it myself."

"Alicia, don't start with me."

She met my eyes, an innocent look on her face. "Whatever do you mean? You don't think Tripp fits the prodigal son narrative?"

"Really, can we talk about something else?"

"So I re-read the passage, and guess what else I noticed?"

"I don't want to hear it, Alicia."

"Glad you asked. You see, there's this other character. An older brother. The father throws a welcome-home party, and the brother refuses to go in! Imagine that!"

I sighed. "If I didn't love you so much, I'd be really mad right now."

"You need to forgive him, Kyle. You've harbored this grudge too long. It's eating away at you."

"*He* needs to ask for forgiveness."

"Why do you think I invited him over?"

"What! When?"

"He's in the living room. Waiting on you."

"Okay, now I *am* mad. You had no right to set this up behind my back."

"I'm your wife and the mother of your child. I have every right. Just talk to him."

Talking to him was the last thing I wanted to do. Why couldn't she stay out of it?

"Kyle, look at me."

"I'm not going out there, Alicia. You asked him here, so you get rid of him."

"It's not just Tripp you need to forgive."

"You're crazy," I said.

"Growing up, you were always your little brother's protector. His life coach. But somehow, you never saw this coming. You couldn't imagine he'd make the same mistakes with Charlotte that you made."

"Worse mistakes."

"True. But it's time to move on. Tripp made his own decisions. This is your chance to put it all behind you. You need to forgive yourself too, Kyle."

"Forgive myself? What's gotten into you?"

The baby gurgled, and she handed me the Bible.

I dropped it on the bed like it was burning my hands. "You know what—I'll talk to him. But after I hear his list of excuses, the only one I'll need to be forgiving is you, for putting me in this situation."

I threw on a pair of jeans and stomped into the living room with my arms crossed.

Tripp stood quickly, fidgeting. New tattoos decorated his arms. Lines on his face betrayed troubled times.

"Howdy." He looked at the floor.

I recalled days we'd spent together catching native cutthroats out of remote glacier lakes. Seemed like another lifetime. And two different people.

"It's been a long time." My voice sounded strange.

"Can we sit? This might take a while."

"Why?"

"I want to tell you everything. And then you can tell me to get lost forever."

Alicia settled into the rocker.

I took a seat in my favorite easy chair next to her. "Go for it."

He cleared his throat and retook his perch on the edge of the sofa. "That day in the conference room. I felt so free when I walked out of there. I'm not like you, Kyle. I hated the ranch. I didn't want to inherit half of it and work there all my life. Charlotte offered me a way out."

"What happened with the startup?"

"It seemed great at first. The investors and me—we threw these lavish parties. I questioned them at first. Seemed too expensive. But Charlotte and the others told me it was the only way to attract high-end investors. And it seemed to be working. Soon I forgot about my misgivings. The parties got crazier, and I got lost in the lifestyle."

"Crazy—like drugs?"

He nodded. "I'm humiliated to think about it now. I have a cocaine addiction, Kyle. I'll be fighting it the rest of my life."

I shook my head. My brother—an addict!

"For a while the profits were good, and the investors happy. But the commercial real-estate market tanked, and we were too highly leveraged to get through it. That means too much debt."

"I know what leveraged means, Tripp."

"Sorry. Anyway, the consortium made me the fall guy. The board voted me out. They gave me a nice severance, but I couldn't hook on anywhere after that. My reputation was shot.

And the severance—well, you can guess what happened to that money."

"I can imagine."

"It was gone in a few months. Charlotte and I hit the streets. A nice lady took us in and lent us some cash. We used it to buy and sell crack. My second sale turned out to be an undercover cop. The lady's money was gone, and I was in jail. Charlotte bailed me out and I never saw her again."

"I'm glad she didn't take the entire twelve grand for herself," I said.

"Twelve grand! How'd you know . . . that was you?"

I nodded. "She threatened to call Pops. He was sick, Tripp. The stress might have killed him."

"Well, regardless of your motivation, I thank you. You saved my life. I couldn't have taken another day in that place. After, I took a plea and got probation."

"You were back on the streets? Alone?"

"I was in and out of rehab. Washing dishes. Cleaning bathrooms. Feeding chickens. Whatever it took to survive. At my lowest, I finally decided to crawl back to Dad, where I'd have a chance to stay sober. I'd clean out latrines, take care of the horses, anything. Unworthy to be called his son, I'd ask him to take me on as a hired hand. The lowest of them lived better than me.

"But before I could get to the door, he ran to me in the driveway. I never got the first word out of my mouth. I didn't expect him to throw me a party."

"Me neither," I said dryly.

"Look, I know I'm also unworthy to be called your brother. But I came here hoping you'd at least find it in your heart to forgive me."

I stood, and Tripp followed my lead. "That's quite a story," I said.

"So, what do you say?"

I glanced at Alicia. Chin up, she gave nothing away. But I knew she'd been right. About everything.

I swiveled back to Tripp. Waited until he lifted his head and looked me in the eyes.

"You had me at 'Howdy,'" I said. "I missed you, Bro."

Tripp's face melted, and he threw his arms around me. My lost brother had been found.

NOVEMBER OR NEVER

By Linda Lyle

When Katherine is abruptly fired from her job, she's encouraged to revisit her long-abandoned dream of writing a novel. This inspirational fiction tackles the themes of self-doubt and the power of friendship and support in times of crisis on the road to self-discovery.

Linda Lyle is an author, knitter, and unintentional collector of cats, who knits together novels with mystery, humor, and romance. Her current releases are a novella collection, *A Christmas by Any Other Name*, and *The 5-Minute Prayer Plan for When Life is Overwhelming*. Both are available on Amazon.

As a freelance writer, Linda has written for Open Windows, Salem Web Network, Refresh Bible Study Magazine, and as a contributor for Lighthouse Bible Studies and SCWC books. Check out all her work and her blog on lindalyle.com, where *The End Of My Yarn* is just the beginning.

"AND THEN SHE said, 'It has nothing to do with your work. You've always gone above and beyond anything you've been asked.'" Katherine Boswell threw a soggy tissue ball toward the trashcan and grabbed more Kleenex from the box. "Rumors circulated about possible downsizing next year, but everyone thought we'd make it through the holidays first. I only had two more months before my 401k would be fully vested so I thought I was safe. And then, boom!"

"That's terrible!" Her friend, Megan, said clearly through the telephone.

"She handed me a folder with some stuff about severance and a generic reference letter and then called someone from security to see me out."

"Typical."

Kat wadded up another tissue and rolled it between her palms, picturing the HR manager's head as a target. "I thought she meant he would walk me to the door, not stand over me while I packed up my office and escort me to the parking lot."

"No way!" Megan sounded as incensed as Kat felt. "What? Were they afraid you would steal a stapler?"

Kat imagined her bestie's face getting as red as her hair. College roommate and friend for life, Megan was the only person she wanted to talk to even though Megan lived in Memphis and Kat's home was north of Birmingham.

She dug the folder with the severance information out of her tote bag and stared at it, forcing herself to breathe.

"According to HR, it is now standard procedure because one person, after being given two weeks' notice, deleted a bunch of important files from the system before they left."

"So, you got escorted out like a criminal?"

"Yep." Kat threw the packet on the kitchen bar and kicked her shoes off. "At least they didn't pat me down before I got in the car."

A strangled sound came from the other end of the line.

She pressed the receiver against her ear. "You okay, Meg?"

"You made me snort my coffee."

Kat laughed, but she could feel the tears welling up again. Determined not to cry over it anymore, even to Megan, she made a lame excuse and prepared to disconnect the call.

"Wait!" Megan practically shouted. "Before you go, let me point out this may finally be the time."

Kat jolted out of her self-pity. "The time for what?"

"To finish that book you started in college."

"Seriously?"

"Yes, seriously." Megan's voice resonated with conviction.

"Talk about a blast from the past . . . ."

"Think about it." Background noise garbled Megan's words. "Well, now I have to go. Kevin needs my help with dinner. Love you."

"Love you, too."

"Don't let this get you down." Megan's line clicked.

Kat shook her head. Writing? She needed a real job with a real income. Her single status meant no one in her own life like Kevin, whose great-paying job could provide a fallback source of support. She was on her own.

Tears trickled down her cheeks. She grabbed a box of tissues and burrowed into her favorite blanket. Within seconds she felt a furry bundle squirm under the cover until it settled behind her knees and began to purr.

"I can always count on you for support, can't I, Shadow? I guess I'm not totally alone after all."

An answering purr almost brought a smile. She reached down and rubbed the cat between his ears and he leaned into her caresses.

She stared at the ceiling. "What am I going to do?"

Eventually Shadow informed her he was hungry. She dished out a bowl of ice cream for herself at the same time she fed him. Not the most nutritious supper she'd ever had, but she couldn't manage anything more substantial.

Tucking herself into bed to snuggle with Shadow again, she closed her eyes and waited for answers. Inspiration failed to strike before she fell into a restless sleep, still hoping for a brighter tomorrow.

When she awoke, rain rather than sunshine streamed on her bedroom window.

"About right."

Shadow sprawled on the couch, half-buried in a blanket. The temptation to join him dragged at her, but yielding to it would get her nowhere fast.

She stretched and yawned. "Well, Mama always said a good night's sleep and a hearty breakfast would set things to right."

Hearty, of course, was limited by the contents of her pantry. She rummaged through the kitchen cabinet. "Do breakfast pastries and coffee count?"

Shadow's ear twitched.

"I didn't think so either, but it will have to do."

She scowled at the folder on the kitchen bar while she savored the honey bun and nursed her coffee to the last dregs. Finally deciding she couldn't postpone any longer, she reached for the folder, but froze with her hand still in mid-air.

"Nope. I have a better idea, Shadow." She left the packet where it was and headed for the shower.

She returned, armored in her favorite caramel-brown and soft-rose outfit, with hair still slightly damp and smelling of shampoo.

Shadow raised one eyebrow and squinted at her. He hadn't moved from his spot on the couch.

She took the hint.

Folder in one hand, and a notebook in the other, Kat went to the spare bedroom, which doubled as her home office. She paused at the entrance and flipped the calendar. She'd been fired on Halloween. How fitting! Especially since the HR lady was such a witch.

She turned on her laptop. First of the month, she ought to look at her bank balance. Or maybe job searches should take priority. But out of habit, she started with her email.

The newest message jumped out at her. *NaNoWriMo.*

Shortly after she graduated, she first signed up for the annual National Novel Writing Month Challenge. Ten years and counting. Every fall she promised herself she'd attempt to write a novel in November, but she'd failed miserably each time.

She poised her finger over the email link, while the embers of hope warred with remembered discouragement.

Shaking her head, she pushed the laptop away to make room on the desk for the dreaded folder. Might as well get it over with.

As she read over the severance package, her anger and anxiety dissolved as she realized downsizing held some advantages over simply being fired.

She grabbed her phone and pressed speed dial. "Megan, I finally read my severance package."

"Aaaand?"

She counted on her fingers, even though her friend couldn't see her. "They are paying me for the two-week notice period, so I will get two more paychecks, not just the final one."

"That's not bad."

"My insurance is paid through the end of the year."

"Even better."

"Plus, they are letting me have my whole 401k as fully vested." She gave a fist pump.

"That's actually a pretty nice package."

She leaned back in her chair, smirking. "I know."

"So, things aren't as dire as you feared." Megan paused. "Have you thought about what you want to do now?"

Kat could hear the question Megan was not asking. She bit her lip. "Well, I considered applying for teaching at some of the local colleges at least part-time, but there won't be any openings until January."

"Meanwhile, you have a nest egg and time on your hands. Whatever could you do with that?" Megan's words oozed snark.

"I know where you're going."

"See how clever you are?"

"I'm not sure if that is the best use of my time."

Megan sighed. "You said it yourself." Her voice took on a practical tone. "You have breathing space and enough money to live on. Haven't you been threatening to try that write-a-novel-in-November thing for the past decade? Why not do it now?"

Kat stiffened. "Are you reading my e-mail?"

"Of course not! Why?"

"Because I just got a message from them about the opening activities that are happening today."

"Perfect!"

Kat moved her phone away from her ear. "You trying to make me deaf?"

"Sorry," Megan said in a slightly lower pitch.

Kat laughed. "I admire your enthusiasm." She switched the phone to speaker and sighed.

"I'm wearing you down, aren't I?" Megan's voice held a tint of the old smugness from college days. Somehow, differences between the two friends always ended with Kat on the proverbial ropes.

Kat closed her eyes and shook her head. "I'll talk to you later."

"Because you have a book to write?"

"Oh, shut up!" She laughed as she disconnected the call and tossed her cellphone aside. She had an email to read.

Kat approached the coffee shop entrance three times before she made it through the door. What a coincidence that her favorite place in Gadsden was hosting a NaNoWriMo event.

Of course, her mother would say there were no coincidences, only God-things.

Kat wasn't sure about that, but she was more comfortable meeting new people in a place she was familiar with, even if the only faces she recognized belonged to the employees.

To her surprise, one of the regular baristas was on the wrong side of the counter.

"Kat?" The young woman waved at her from a table where two other people also sat, laptops open. "Are you here for NaNoWriMo?"

"Yeah."

Jasmine motioned at the empty seat next to her. "Great. You can be our fourth."

"I didn't know you were a writer." Kat put her tote bag on the chair and dug out her own computer before she sat.

"Same." Jasmine grinned. "It's nice to be on this side of the counter for once. I'm so excited. It's my first time to get to try this."

"Me, too."

The speaker across from Kat smiled at them both. "It's our third, so we'd be happy to help you ladies." He touched his chest and then indicated the other man.

Kat nodded at him in acknowledgement, fighting to hide her surprise. Even though he was seated, she could tell he was extremely tall—like, NBA-star-tall. Not to mention good-looking.

"Sorry, Rick." Jasmine gave an endearingly crooked smile. "Kat, this is Rick Finnigan."

He reached across the table and shook Kat's hand.

Jasmine motioned to the guy to Kat's right. "And this is Paul Phillips."

The other man dipped his head in friendly greeting.

Near the front of the room, someone clapped their hands. "Attention, everyone!"

A soft-spoken facilitator welcomed the NaNoWriMo group and gave some quick writing tips and ideas. Once the formalities were out of the way, the leader smiled. "Now, you've found your tribe. Take a couple minutes to introduce yourselves, find ways to support each other for the rest of the month, and remember, if you're not having fun, you're probably not doing it right."

A couple of extroverts whooped. Most of the other writers chuckled. Kat just took a deep breath.

As the room settled into a low hubbub of quiet conversation, Kat looked around the table. Someone else had better speak up, because her reservoir of courage had run out.

Paul leaned in and pitched his voice low. "We already caught up with each other. Kat, what's your novel about? Is anything giving you trouble?"

She shrugged. "Other than I have no idea what it is about?"

The other three laughed, but then took turns asking questions about her story. As Kat responded to their prompts, a visual of her main character crystallized in her mind's eye, and she even gained understanding of plot points like "greatest desire" and "blind spots." Soon her fingers flew over the keyboard with a flurry of notes and ideas.

They took turns brainstorming around the table. Simply talking about other people's work gave her more insight into her own. She had never experienced this kind of interaction before. Neither her college friends nor her old co-workers understood the ins and outs of writing the way these fellow authors did. Her pulse raced, she rubbed her hands with glee, and optimism drove out her post-downsizing blues.

More quickly than she would have believed, the facilitator announced the event was over. "I know you could keep writing all night, but the folks at the coffee shop are about to lock up and kick us out. And we want to be able to come back next Monday evening for week two!"

A flurry of activity ensued. Tote bags and briefcases swallowed laptops and notebooks. Empty coffee cups and paper plates disappeared into trash cans. Jasmine circulated throughout the room, giving tabletops a swish and a shine with a handy spray bottle and a clean tea towel.

Kat hesitated. She cleared her throat. "So, do y'all meet here every Monday to do a review of the previous week?"

Paul nodded. "Rick and I do. Jasmine's usually catching 40 winks by that time of night, since she works the early shift. You're welcome to join us."

"I'm in." Kat squared her shoulders.

"Looking forward to it." Rick leaned in where only she could hear. He smiled and gave a wave before disappearing into the crowd.

Kat sighed and picked up her computer bag.

"I think somebody has a crush." Jasmine's eyes twinkled.

"I barely know him." Kat tucked an errant hair behind her ear, fighting to keep the color from rising in her cheeks.

"I meant Rick, but okay." The barista jostled Kat with her elbow. "See you next week."

As the month flew by, Kat faithfully logged her NaNoWriMo sessions on a calendar. Some days were over in a blink, while others felt like they would never end. She wrote 5,000 words in a single session—although she deleted most of them later—but the next time she sat down at her keyboard, she struggled for an hour to write a single five-word sentence. Timely emails from the main NaNo account urged her not to quit in the middle of the project. And her new friends helped her through trouble spots during their Monday night meetings.

Despite taking some time out for the holidays, on the twenty-ninth, Kat was less than 5,000 words short of the word count goal that once seemed insurmountable.

A text from Rick popped on her phone. *Don't forget our final meeting is 7pm tomorrow. You can do it! 30 days of great writing!*

She gave a wry chuckle and sent a reply. *Your writing may be great. Not too sure about mine.*

I am. He punctuated it with a heart-eyes emoji.

Before she could respond, he added, *Can't wait to see you.* Along with two more heart-eyes.

Ditto. She gathered her courage and added the same emoji before she pressed the Send button.

Newly energized, she stayed up until midnight to finish her story. She passed the threshold of the required word count two sentences before the final denouement.

Giddy, she whooped when she typed "The End." Her heart pounded as she uploaded the last of her novel to the NaNoWriMo website and received a message confirming validation of her project completion. Just before exhaustion tipped the scales over elation, she burrowed into her pillow and murmured, "Megan, you were right."

The final event, on November 30th, held fewer people than the opening, but that wasn't the only difference. This time, Kat was part of the camaraderie and community, no longer a newbie. Still, she made a beeline for her group of friends as soon as the barista made her latte.

"I can't believe we all finished our novels." Jasmine held up her coffee cup. "Cheers to us."

Kat saluted with her latte and took a sip.

"Well, I had a head start." Paul raised his cup but didn't drink. "I used the 10,000 words I finished last time."

"Same here." Rick nodded toward Kat. "You, on the other hand, rocked it."

"I did reuse 3,000 words from back in the day." Kat flushed. "My college professor, a published novelist, told us we should never throw anything away."

"Still, you finished your first novel, and that is an accomplishment." Rick smiled and touched his cup to hers as formally as if they were champagne flutes.

"First novel?" Her cheeks burned hotter. "You mean my only novel?"

"I seriously doubt that." Jasmine shook her head, smiling. "It's really good."

They chattered on for a while glorying in completing the challenge, but mostly excited that it was over. Their conversation was interrupted by a shrill whistle coming from the front of the room so the area leader could give closing remarks.

While everyone else was listening to the facilitator, Rick pulled her toward a quiet corner. "Would you like to go out with me to dinner tomorrow to celebrate?"

Kat looked over at the other two members of the group.

He leaned closer. "Just the two of us."

"I'd like that." She smiled.

As soon as she got home, Kat called Megan. "You won't believe what happened. I finished my novel, and Rick asked me out!"

Megan's squeal made Kat wince and move the phone away from her ear, but she laughed.

"It's good to hear you laugh again."

"I laugh."

"Not like that and not in a long time, and I don't just mean because of Rick." Megan chuckled. "Don't get me wrong. It's nice that you found someone, but you were never this happy at your old job or even teaching before that. I really think you have found your calling."

Kat flopped on the sofa. "I wish. But I can't make a living at this. It feels great to finally finish this novel, but how am I going to afford food and rent?"

"Other people do it. There must be a way."

Silence hung in the air while Kat waited for her friend to conjure an answer.

She sighed. "Look, it's been a long month and an even longer night. I'm going to hit the hay."

"Just think about it. And sleep well."

December first brought no more answers. Fortified with coffee, she started a job search on the internet. Nothing looked remotely interesting. She was going to have to make some decisions soon. Her last paycheck had come and gone, and unemployment was not enough to live on for very long.

Shadow danced across her keyboard, head-butting her.

"Are you telling me it's time for a break?" She lured the cat into her arms and snuggled him against her shoulder. She got up and walked to the window, gazing at the familiar scene. "What am I going to do, Shadow?"

An idea for a new novel coalesced, images forming in her head. Giving her furry friend one final scritch, she released him so she could rummage through the desk drawer for a notebook.

Shadow followed her to the living room. When she settled on the sofa, he perched on the arm on her left, in his favorite "pet me" spot. She obliged with one hand but used the other to scribble down notes as quickly as the ideas germinated. "Just because I can't make a living out of it doesn't mean I can't keep writing, right?"

Shadow purred in response, eyes half closed in bliss.

Several pages later, her brainstorm slowed to a drizzle, but the rough shell of a story idea had taken shape. When the doorbell took her by surprise, she glanced at the clock. "Time flies, Shadow. My date's here!"

Rick smiled in appreciation as soon as she came through the front entrance. He walked her to his SUV and waited while she fastened her seatbelt, then closed her door gently before getting in the other side and starting the engine. "So, what is your next step?"

"With what?"

"Your writing, silly. What else?"

She squirmed against the leather upholstery. "It was a wild ride, but now I have to get back to the real world."

"Why?"

"I have bills to pay. Rent. And I'm addicted to eating regularly." She stared at his profile.

His lips quirked in the ghost of a smile. "You can make a living as an author. Maybe novels won't bring in immediate cash, but there are lots of way to earn money writing."

"Like what?"

"Freelancing pays the bills for a lot of people. I have a contact at a local magazine that fits with your background. That would get you started. I'll give you the info, and you can send them a query letter."

"Isn't that just a waste of time? I feel I should be applying for stable jobs."

"Tell you what. Do both." He gave her a side glance. "See what happens."

Her stomach did a backflip. "I'll think about it."

He grinned. "That's all I'm asking."

When he dropped her off later that night, he left her at the door with tingling lips and a card with the editor's contact information.

For the first time in her adult life, she didn't call Megan the minute she got home from a date, because she had something even more important than spilling the tea to her best friend. She had a query to send and a new career to begin.

RISING SUBLIME

By Thom Brucie

In this literary fiction, Clovis faces loss and other personal struggles in a dry, desolate land where it hasn't rained in years.

Thom Brucie's novel, *Children of Slate*, won the 2023 bronze medal Illumination Award for excellence in Catholic literature, and his novel, *Obsidian Mirth*, won the American Writing Award in fiction (2022) and was short-listed for the Hawthorne Prize. His poetry chapbook, *Apprentice Lessons*, earned the 2024 Miriam Chaikin Award in Poetry, and his chapbook *Moments Around The Campfire with A Vietnam Vet* was named the best chapbook of 2010 and is a finalist for the American Legacy Award in Poetry, 2024.

Thom's short stories and poems have appeared in a variety of journals, including *The San Joaquin Review*, *Cappers*, *The Southwestern Review*, *Pacific Review*, *Wilderness House Literary Review*, *North Atlantic Review*, and many others. Learn more about it at thombrucie.com.

Rising Sublime

THE OLD MAN who sold him the beer told him it hadn't rained in years.

"Years?" Clovis asked.

"Yes, sir. That's why ain't nobody left but me."

"Years," Clovis repeated. "I don't know how anything can go dry that long."

"Can't say to that," the old man admitted. "I can tell ya that the last time it rained, Margaret was still here."

"Margaret?"

"My Margaret."

"What happened?"

"Stopped raining. Then it got lonely."

Clovis nodded. "I understand loneliness," he said. "What do I owe you?"

The old man looked around the store. "Was a gas station once," he said. "This is what's left."

Clovis held his wallet open.

"How much you got in there?" the old one asked.

"Not much."

"You got fifty?"

"For a six-pack of beer?"

"For the whole place. Time for me to move on. Ain't seen rain in years."

"I don't want your store. Just some beer. I'm movin' on, too."

"No, sir, you ain't ready. Give me that five spot."

Clovis handed him the bill.

The old man took the money, put on his hat, and walked out the door.

Clovis took the six-pack and followed. He leaned against the front wall, popped a can, and watched the old man walk away. The long, empty road spread like a thin wing. One side, ribboning to his right, lay like an impassive macadamed flatbread left too long in the sun. To his left, it rose up a slight ridge and vanished into the distance.

By the time the old man disappeared behind the ridge, the sun left for twilight, and Clovis fell asleep on the gray boards of the walkway.

When he awakened, he sat up and rubbed his back muscles against the wall of the abandoned station. He slapped the dust from his sleeves, raising a light chalky shadow that floated like talcum toward the rusted metal overhang. He passed that day alone, on an old wooden walkway, in a waterless land, and nothing changed except that the sun set and rose again the next day, and set again, and rose again each day after that, all days, all time unchanging.

Forty days passed. Forty times the sun rose, crossed the sky, and set. Forty times the moon came and went, covering the earth with white dryness. Each day dragged on toward night in an endless drudgery of dreary monotony. The only sound of time passing was the wind scratching against the arid sand, like a lost hope uttered into a whisper. The old man said it hadn't rained in years, and Clovis did not want to admit it, but he knew this to be true. The days and the nights passed like a ceaseless discontent he could not subsume.

On the morning of the forty-first day, a murky haze, like a gauze curtain, sheltered the horizon against the brewing yeast of another sweltering day. The rising air stirred as if water boiling, and the vapor made the roadway glisten. He raised his hand in salutation to the sun's emergence, and between the shadow of his fingers he saw something move within the road shimmer, too far away to identify, but definitely a life form.

The creature wandered off the road and back again, crossing and zigzagging. Clovis identified the thing as a dog.

He watched the dog close in, its pointed snout sniffing, its eyes darting, until it noticed Clovis, and it stopped. They looked at one another, one uncertainty paralleling the other.

Clovis raised the can and sipped. The dog, as if in response to the gesture, walked toward him. It was a medium-sized dog, thirty-five maybe forty pounds. It stepped onto the wooden walkway and sat, chin up, looking directly at Clovis. The dog was a female, and she had blue eyes.

"Do you have a name?"

The dog did not change expression, but it did relax a little.

"You need a name, of course, if we're going to talk. What's a good name for a girl dog? I know. I'll call you Margaret, for the old man. His Margaret. His love."

Clovis relaxed then, too. He leaned against the wall and stretched his legs.

"So, Margaret, what's a nice girl like you doing in a place like this?" He closed his eyes. Memory rose up behind them.

"Her name was Laura, and I actually said that to her. In the backyard, near the fence." He looked at the dog. "You sure you want to hear this? It's getting hot, and you must be tired."

The dog rested its chin on its paws.

"Okay," Clovis said. "By the way, Margaret, there's beer if you're thirsty."

Margaret, the dog, got up and went to the store entrance. She pulled open the door and went in. She returned with two cans of beer and set them on the walkway. Clovis took one and pulled the cap. He set it down in front of Margaret. She nosed it onto its side and drank the contents as it spilled.

Clovis popped his can and continued.

"We met at my Aunt Sylvia's house. We were eleven. That's eleven human years by the way, not dog years. We always went to visit Aunt Sylvia at Christmas time. Laura's family had just moved into the house next door.

What do you mean by a place like this?

It's kind of a joke.

What kind of joke?

I'm not really sure. My cousin, Nick, he told me. It's what he says.

I don't understand, so it's not a funny joke.

"Then we ate ice cream. That's it. How we met."

Clovis kept his eyes shut. He could see the past better with them closed. Nearly forgotten memories re-shaped, like scrubbed marble buffed bright and clean. Enraptured in the melancholia of the past, he exhaled a sound, like a sigh of dry lament.

"I kissed her, you know. Well, I kissed her a lot, but our first kiss happened that Christmas at Aunt Sylvia's. Aunt Sylvia's holiday decorations always included a sprig of green mistletoe hung in the doorway to the living room.

Understand, Margaret, if two humans accidently meet under mistletoe, they must kiss. It's a rule of magic. I know dogs don't have magic. You don't need to remind me. I know. Dogs lay around. Sniff stuff."

He opened his eyes and looked at Margaret. She lay, like a dog, transfixed and unmoving.

"I hardly know you, and, yet, you behave like you know me. How can a dog make such a decision based on no evidence? How do you know you can trust me? You don't know. You hope, though. Right? It's not magic for you. It's instinct.

"Mistletoe only grows in shaded forest areas. And it only grows in the branches of trees. Its roots grow in the air, not in dirt. So you see, Margaret, it's a rare phenomenon since its roots are not bound to the earth. Magic, see?

"After we ate, people milled around getting ready to say good-bye. I went looking for a last piece of pie. Just as I walked into the living room doorway, Laura, carrying a piece of pumpkin pie on a paper plate, came around the corner, and we met under the mistletoe. Can you picture us? Struggling with approaching adolescence, heavy with Christmas magic, and caught in the adult trap of mistletoe?

"We knew we had to kiss. That's how humans are, Margaret. They want to kiss, but they're afraid. Afraid to touch because if you touch someone, you feel it past your skin. It seeps inside of you, and it makes you thirsty for tenderness."

Clovis caught Margaret looking at him, her blue eyes expectant.

"You're a good dog, Margaret."

Margaret took a step toward him. She leaned her snout up to his face and stared at him, at his eyes.

Clovis reached out and touched the dog.

"It was like that," he said to her. "The eyes. Dogs, they don't have pretense. If they like you, they say so with the eyes. Not humans. Humans use their eyes to pretend. It's too much work, loving, so you hide kindness behind indifference. Well, you don't. You're a dog. But people do. But we didn't. When we looked into one another's eyes, we saw each other. Then we kissed."

He paused to endure the thorny ache of yearning.

"I wish I could describe that kiss. That inexperienced, willful act of courage. Yes, courage, Margaret, because truth overcame us. We each declared with our eyes—this is who I am. It is a rare gift to share your true self. Scary, because what if she rejects you? But she did not reject me. She accepted me. I tell you, Margaret, I miss her. Here, in my head, and here, in my heart."

The memory quickened against his eyes, and he squeezed the lids to bind it. Margaret moved closer and placed her head on his leg. Clovis rested his hand on her fur.

"We fell in love that day. We did not know, of course, we were too young. But that kiss, that magic, brought us together, and from that moment we were no longer alone. Imagine, Margaret, not being alone."

He stroked her rough fur, and the dog accepted the affection.

"You and I were alone, and now we are not. You are kind to share time with me, but you are not Laura. No one else is Laura.

"Our youthful years were uneventful, except that all through school everyone knew we were paired. Even through the joyride of adolescence, we grew closer. Everyone knew we would get married, and we did.

"A June bride. Of course, a June bride. Humans do things like that, Margaret, explain magic through ceremony. June is the bride's month. It's high summer. Nature has blossomed and fruited. Birds and trees, rabbits and flowers. All of life is alive and healthy. A bride's time of vitality and optimism. We had white lilies."

Clovis stopped talking. He held the dog, and her fur grew wet with his tears.

"She was not healthy. She did not know. We did not know. Why did no one know? It's not fair. What could I do? An aneurism. Do you know what that is, Margaret? Me neither. Something inside the body breaks, cracks open. You know, it leaks. Then the brain turns off, shuts down. And the body follows. Stops talking. Stops smiling. Stops seeing."

He cried then with the forlorn grief of a man who has lost his way, a man isolated and unrooted. He whispered her name, "Laura," into the quiet of exhaustion, and he fell asleep.

Sleep heals. That's its job. And Clovis the sleeper slept the sleep of dreams.

He startled awake, and he met Margaret's stare.

"I had a dream. I'm riding a great rhinoceros into a cave. He charges headlong, armor clanging against the enclosing walls. The walls are like a funnel, growing smaller and smaller, until we reach a tunnel. The beast cannot continue for its size. I jump off and run into the opening that leads downward into the abyss. The empty blackness makes all thought incomprehensible. Dread seizes me, and I tremble with terror, unable to move."

Clovis breathed quickly, still caught in the night tremors. The terror of the dream clung to Clovis like heat, and Margaret waited while Clovis regained some composure.

"It's a hero quest, you think? Fierce beast. Clanging armor. Running into danger. But I ask you, what sort of hero finds himself within a black fear, unable to move? Perhaps it is the furious ride of the rhinoceros which exhausts me."

Clovis leaned against the old structure, puzzled.

"What then? The fear? It is the fear that exhausts me? No, that cannot be. Fear cannot be the cause of fear, can it?"

That long day, Clovis sat in the silent heat, unmoving, unable to clear his mind, unable to dictate the rhythms of his heart. Eventually, cautiously, into the deep black of the night he slept. And he dreamed again.

The next morning, Clovis revealed to Margaret. "I had that dream again, but something changed. Really. Yes truly. Okay, I'll tell you.

"I rode the rhinoceros to the abyss as before. Dread and terror held me, but instead of waking, I peered into the nothingness. In the distance, I saw the lake of the dead.

"Of course it has significance. Aren't we all going to die one day? At this point, however, I don't know what significance.

"I braved the darkness until I reached the edge of the water. The lake was filled with heads of the dead. One of them floated over to me. It was the ancient head of Atlas. You know Atlas, right? Carried the weight of the world on his shoulders, the ponderous weight of life and death, of history and oblivion? That's news to you? It means he bears the weight of what is remembered and what is forgotten. Nevertheless, let me continue.

"The panic in my face must have shown because the head of Atlas said, 'Calm yourself.' I felt his ancient voice, a voice like a mountain of stone, profound and living. I knew that voice, that living mountain, inside me.

"You think that's one of those adjustments of re-awakening? Why? A dead lake and a living mountain you say. Like the death of an old idea and re-birth into a larger world? I don't know. Maybe."

Margaret brought two beers and sat down to listen, but Clovis could find no more to say. A tenuous silence encased them.

"I wish you wouldn't interrupt my thinking, Margaret. What do you want? I don't care if you need to pee. Go. No, I won't miss you. Wait. I'll go with you. Don't want you to get lost. Don't say that. I am not the one who is lost."

They walked to the side of the old building. The urine sizzled as it hit the hot sand. The area dried quickly and left no residue, as if it detested memory of any sort. The day dragged on, as days before. It dragged into the evening, and eventually it dragged into the somber silence of the darkening night. Encumbered with a burden of accumulating foreboding, Clovis finally fell asleep.

That night, Clovis dreamed his terrorizing dream again.

On the morning of the third day, the sun rose, as it will do in spite of dreams. Margaret waited on the walkway. Without introduction, Clovis began.

"The dream, Margaret," he said. "Something new again. Yes, I'll tell you. Atlas told me to open the egg at my feet. I cracked the shell, and a white dove flew over the lake, its glow illuminating all. The water of death was calm and red, and

Laura's death mask floated toward me. She looked up at the dove. I looked too. Together we watched the dove transform into a chalice. It floated down and hovered between us, between Laura and me. Laura looked away from the chalice and turned her face to me. Then she closed her eyes, and her head sank into the red depths. Again, I heard the somber voice of Atlas. 'The cup you are offered bids a choice.'

"Of course I know the obvious interpretation. You don't have to tell me. I know. I know I must allow Laura to settle into the peaceful sleep of afterlife. That's it, right? Yet, I resist."

He looked at the dog.

"She died in the hospital. Sterile fluorescent white lights. Disinfected machines. Stainless steel rails on the bed. A bleak, impersonal, frigid box. I held her, warm and soft. At the end, I felt her soul release from her body, rising up, away from me, out of the frigidity of the sterile room and into the numinous afterlife. But I did not let go.

"Of course I expected her to still be alive. Wouldn't you? Don't look at me that way, Margaret. I know what you're thinking. But I can't, I tell you. I cannot let go of her."

This last he shouted, and the dog backed away from him.

Clovis raised the can to drink, but he stopped. The can became a question in his hand. Half empty or half full? The can bespoke the perilous razor's edge of change, and Clovis pondered the half-empty/half-full quandary of choice.

Clovis looked at Margaret.

"What do you think I should do?" he asked. "Oh, now you keep quiet, now, when I need you. I tell you, Margaret, I'm confused. I don't know what to do, and I don't know how to do it. Can love hold its value as a memory?

"What do you mean, think of Atlas? That he is not the master of who is remembered and who is forgotten. He is only the bearer of this weight. So you say. Tell me, who, then, is the master?"

This question sank into Clovis's heart and settled with a thud.

He turned away from the dog, and he raised the beer can. "You!" he shouted into the sky. "I'm tired of symbols. Tell me what I mean." It was a shout of trepidation, and he glared at the can.

"Okay, I'll try to see it as half-full."

He had yet to discover what fruit a small act of courage might yield, but taking a step into the unknown, he threw the half-full can into the dusty air.

He watched as the can spun in an arc, whirling as if electrified, causing the spray to spiral in the arched pattern of a sunrise rainbow, droplets tumbling and glistening like fireflies. As the exhausted can landed, a distant thunder rumbled through the hills against the far horizon. A growing echo extended for several long seconds, coalescing into a deafening blast that pounded open the sky and triggered a bulbous cloud encumbered with rain.

And it rained upon the stillness.

Clovis looked at Margaret. "I don't know," he said, half a statement, half a question.

As the rain continued, the old man appeared atop the rise in the road. He trudged through the deluge and onto the wooden walkway. He took off his hat, wiped the rain from his face, and sat next to Clovis.

"Did you find Margaret?" Clovis asked.

"Of course not," the old man said. "Found myself. You ready to sell this place?"

"Sell?"

"Yes, sir. Time you was movin' on."

"I'm not going anywhere," Clovis said.

"It's time for your journey."

"The same journey you went on?"

"Your own journey," the old one said. "I'll give you three dollars."

"I paid you five. I'll lose money."

"With every loss, a lesson."

The old man handed Clovis three dollars. Margaret the dog rested its muzzle on the old man's lap.

"Named her Margaret, you say? For me? That's a fine gift. I'll remember you for it."

Clovis took a cautious step off the wooden planks onto the re-awakened earth, and fighting the urge to look backwards, he walked onward into a gently gathering day.

"A rhinoceros, you say?" the old man said to the dog. "Never heard that one before."

RENEWAL

By Erin Jamieson

This psychological narrative explores the internal struggles of eating disorders and their impacts. Hope and acceptance can only be derived from a shift in mindset.

Erin Jamieson is published in over 100 literary magazines, including two Pushcart Prize nominations.

Her poetry chapbook, *Fairytales*, was published by Bottlecap Press. Her most recent chapbook, *Remnants*, came out in 2024, and her debut novel, *Sky of Ashes, Land of Dreams*, was published by Type Eighteen Books.

EVERYONE WANTED ME to eat lunch.

We had to wait a few hours for a bed, which meant I would miss when they'd usually be serving me—or as I thought of it—*feeding* me.

Mom and Dad brought up soup and sandwiches from the hospital's food court. Cheesy soup, some kind of club sandwich, and an Asian wrap, which I remember came with peanut sauce. I would have eaten something similar in the past, and I think that's what Mom had in mind when she ordered it for me.

Even though it smelled delicious, even though I was hungry, even though it had been hours since I'd last eaten . . . I shoved the food aside. I told them that I didn't want it, although I really meant I didn't know how many calories it had, which really meant I had already had my vegetables and hard-boiled egg earlier and I didn't feel I had earned any more food yet.

It's hard to explain to anyone, like you, who has never had an eating disorder, but that's how I thought of it. Food had to be earned, through exercise. But even a long run would not have been enough, at that moment, to allow myself to eat more than a bite.

Looking back now, it was early into my eating disorder. Mom and Dad got so angry. So frustrated with me.

"Don't you know they're going to make you eat?"

"Don't you know you're killing yourself?"

I walked away from both of them, toward the window. By no stretch of the imagination could it be called a nice view. We were several stories up, and all I could see were more gray concrete rooms across from us, and a parking lot that felt large enough to swallow me whole. Rain fell from a cold gray November sky, and the world felt listless and strange. I watched a woman get out of her car, open an umbrella, and lead a child by the hand.

I remember wondering what it would feel like to jump. I've always been afraid of heights. So it's not that I really intended to jump. I just thought about it. I imagined getting up on the windowsill. But it is harder, far harder, to imagine the actual fall—how fast or slow it would seem, if I would have time to process what was happening. If it would hurt, or if there would not be time to think about that.

Mom tried to get me to eat more.

"At least drink something."

The first several nights the heart monitor went off often, when my pulse plunged too low. I cannot remember what it dropped to, (a blessing), only that it was low enough I knew there was a chance I might die. The first several days, too, as they tried to increase my calories, I started getting refeeding syndrome for the first time in all the years I'd had an eating disorder. My electrolytes dipped so I had to take supplements. It took a few days for things to stabilize, and even then, they had to proceed with caution.

The swelling in my legs, which I didn't even realize I had until I was hospitalized, reduced over the first day. Progress was slow, and the decision of what to do for treatment was looming over me the entire stay. The doctors insisted on residency, after my heart rate went up enough, but Mom wanted me to go back to the local inpatient.

I felt ashamed that I'd gotten in this mess again. I felt even worse when Angie, a nurse who I always found a bit authoritarian and a tad harsh, who knew me from my previous visits, started to talk with me on a personal level she never had before.

"You can't do this again. You know that, right?"

She wasn't talking about that particular day . . . she wasn't even referring to the fact that that hospital wouldn't take me again.

She knew there was a chance that, if there was a next time, I might die.

She shared with me that her own daughter had anorexia for many years. She told me how her daughter had to eventually decide for herself.

And in that moment, it all came together—her hawklike eyes, her insistence for protocol and having meals even ahead of schedule—all the things I hated. She was working in this ward because she knew what an eating disorder was like, at least from a mother's perspective.

I was playing some form of solitaire, and, against protocol, she let me eat my snack while I played—albeit with very watchful eyes. And in that moment, the nurse I'd dreaded became a nurse who seemed to care more about me than all the other nurses combined.

I didn't tell you about this. It wasn't to keep it from you, but some things maybe are not meant to be—or cannot be—shared.

It would be several days more before I left, because my heart rate was being stubborn, but as I started to consider my options for the next step in treatment, I became increasingly aware of the fact that I would end up making a decision that would prove controversial.

I did talk to you about that. I talked to you because you had been there for me, just like a number of good friends, through all of this. I talked to you not because you understood my disorder but because you didn't shun or dismiss my thoughts. I talked to you because I was not worried about being judged.

From the beginning, you also seemed to think residential was the best option—not so much because of it being residential as much as following the doctor's logic. Inpatient hadn't worked; outpatient hadn't worked.

"But what if this doesn't work?"

"How do you know it won't?"

I sat up in bed—I was always moving around in that bed, as much as I could, in part to avoid bed sores and in part because I literally couldn't stand being still too long. "Mom doesn't want me to go."

You paused. "Does that matter?"

When I finally went to residential treatment, after all of those bleak years in and out of inpatient and back to constantly changing outpatient teams, I felt guilty. I felt guilty because for the first time, I was around a group of women for whom it was more common to have been emotionally abused than it was not.

In some of the groups, excellent as they were, I did not say much. I remember one group in particular, art therapy. We were supposed to make collages about our eating disorders. I'd never been asked to do something like this before, probably because in inpatient we weren't allowed to have any magazines that might be considered triggering. We weren't allowed to talk about much at all, which is kind of funny when you think about it.

This approach was more daring, more risky. But most people that go to residential need it badly, and trying something new, after other failed attempts at treatment, I guess makes sense in a way.

That day was hard for everyone. But when I made my collage, I saw how stereotypical, so to speak, my eating disorder story was: varsity athlete, perfectionist, sensitive, honor roll student, pushed to succeed.

We were allowed to opt out of sharing, even though I could tell the art therapist was disappointed with me.

The next time, we made T-shirts. We were only told that we were supposed to depict our hurt or pain or anger or regret —in short, any strong negative emotions that we felt held us captive.

I didn't know what to do, and it's not that I didn't have pain, it's that—for once—I didn't know how to express it. The funny thing is, even though this was not all that long ago— five years now, I think—it feels like a lifetime ago but it also feels like it just happened and I am still in that nightmare, those awful long years. And I cannot for the life of me remember what I did end up designing on that T-shirt.

What I do remember is the women who mapped out stories of assault, of abuse. I remember hearing from women who'd spent their lives feeling unloved, with absent or neglectful family, with friends who steered them wrong, with men—many of them friends or partners—who hurt them in ways you never completely forget.

I watched. Some cried. Some did nothing at all. All of them had suffered infinitely more than I ever had, and maybe more than I could have imagined. I sat in the group listening until I started to zone out, as if my own mind was protecting me.

Later, during dinner, I still didn't speak. We were all quiet even though we normally played word games or at least got pretty chatty. The nurse didn't push, and neither did the dietician.

But my silence continued. I spoke less and less in group, until Matt pulled me aside into the "conference center," the room with sun windows and an art supply cabinet and little kitchenette that we used for art therapy and yoga sessions. He asked what was going on, and I admitted I didn't feel like I deserved to be there.

Matt just looked at me.

"Why do you think your pain is any less valid?"

There were a million reasons to answer that. Because, compared to what everyone else had experienced, my pain and struggles were nothing. Because I felt like I'd had a good life and I'd messed it up.

He didn't press any further, because that wasn't the way he did things. We stood up and walked back over to the main house, out on the gravel path, past the garden that was replete with kale and little else. Inside, everyone else was preparing their afternoon snacks. The last thing I wanted to do was eat, but at that moment there was little fear about how much I had to eat and everything to do with feeling like there was nothing more I wanted to do other than sleep for a very long time.

I did what I had to. I prepared my snack. I ate, mechanically, as I had when I first arrived. Outside the sky was chalky gray, the way it was most days in Half Moon Bay and the entire Bay Region, as far as I could tell.

But that day was different, the way the air filled with tension, the way any small disturbance felt monumental, as if we were all waiting for something to happen. Later, we were told to go back and get our T-shirts. Most of us had used hand paint and left them to dry over chairs.

We could do whatever we wanted with the shirts, but most of the women decided to cut them up, bit by bit. It was supposed to be symbolic, of course, and you'd think that would be weird or cheesy, but most of us were crying.

To us, it both meant everything and nothing. I don't think I'm making much sense, but nothing can describe that evening.

Why should your pain be any less valid?

I cut my T-shirt tentatively, then in strips. I did not pay attention to anyone else after a while. With every cut, I felt the pain from the past and the pain now. I felt everything at once —all of those lost years, all of those years not wanting to wake up, all those years feeling like a worthless failure.

I started crying without realizing I was crying, and I didn't stop.

I couldn't stop—because I had finally found a place I could cry, where no one would insist I stop or feel better. I finally was able to be and feel whatever I wanted to, even if at that point I was not sure what that meant.

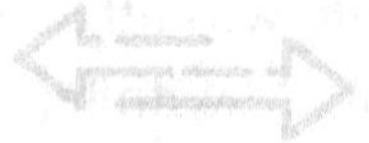

We all want to believe in new beginnings.

A way to reset, start fresh. But one thing I think a lot of us overlook? In order to have a new beginning, something has to change.

It's been years since my stay at residential. Years of fighting my mind, fighting my body. Nothing as severe as when I had to be hospitalized. Because now, when I stumble, I try not to invalidate my pain. I try to understand it.

I understand in a way I thought I never would.

Yet.

There are still gaping wounds, wounds that keep opening, wounds that won't quite close. A sense of restlessness. A longing for something more than mere survival.

I think it's hard to recognize when your life changes. Of course there are obvious markers: a birth, a death (and yes, a marriage). But most of the time we are either changing or resisting change, and it's really those daily choices, those incremental shifts, that add up.

Before I developed a full-blown eating disorder, I told myself, a little more every day, that there was something wrong with my body.

Before you shut yourself off from our family, you told yourself every day that there was a lot to resent.

We rarely change in one day, but we make steps towards it —whether we are aware of it or not. In treatment, I had to eat every day to get closer to being functional again, even though the process was long and frightening and at times almost felt unbearable.

The thing is, as much control as I always want to have over my life, it's hard when you can't foresee the long-term consequences of every little decision you make.

But what I am aware of is this—it feels like I am at a crossroads, and things could go one way or the other.

It feels like a new day.

Spring is in full bloom. Trees of white blossoms line the streets. Tulips are appearing in our disorganized gardens. More neighbors venture out to mow their lawns. The weather is warm enough that last night I had to open up my window.

It's the time of year for fresh beginnings. And strangely, I woke today feeling just that, a feeling of hope I cannot explain. Maybe it will fade as the day wears on. I am still worried about this summer, about my future. I am still haunted by the loss of too many relationships.

I sent you a small thank you for my birthday gift. You never responded, but it was something I needed to do. Despite not getting into any graduate programs, I am publishing as much as I can. Despite having days I feel I would like nothing more than to give up, I don't.

I don't know if we'll ever reunite or not. I know some of this is my fault, and I don't think I've been honest about that. Maybe I should have tried harder to reach out to you after Christmas. You leaving was not my fault, but maybe not trying was.

It's a season of renewal.

I used to think that renewal was an act or a destination, but now I know it is a process. That's what we're all doing, or striving to—renewing ourselves and pruning off the dead parts, letting go of past hurts rather than risk never growing.

I almost died a few times, but Spring has always been a season where I've found my strength again. And every time, I learned something new about myself and those I love.

I don't know what this year will hold, and that terrifies me. But maybe that is the only thing I can do now—to surrender what I cannot control, to try to trust God with the rest.

And to fight for what I believe to be true.

It's April, a time for renewal. A time to learn how to live and forgive again.

And in my mind I still see the sunset Mom pointed out last night, that endless array of crimson and blush, how impossible it was to see where it ended, and how glorious it was to believe, if only for a moment, that it never would.

A CRAZY LITTLE THING CALLED LOVE

By Paula Peckham

Robin lives a mundane and financially strained life in San Francisco. When a stranger reveals hidden details of her past, she is able to piece together the puzzle, which leads to an emotional revelation of familial love and connection in this work of contemporary women's fiction.

Paula Peckham is a fifth-generation Texan. She published her first novel in 2022, and now has three novels and two anthologies to her name.

Her debut novel, *Protected*, Book 1 in The San Antonio series, was published in April 2022. It reached the finals in the American Christian Fiction Writers' Genesis contest and won the gold medal in the 2022 Global Book Awards. Book 2 in the series, *A Father's Gift*, finished third in the 2023 Selah contest. Book 3, *Accepted*, released in October 2023, reached the finals in the Selah contest and won first place in The Bookfest Awards. She is currently working on a contemporary romance titled *Still Haven't Found What I'm Looking For*.

Paula divides her time between her home in Texas and Rio Bravo, Mexico. Look for her on Facebook, Instagram, TikTok, and paulapeckham.com.

Real people with real-life struggles.

A Crazy Little Thing Called Love

"Who died?" My tone revealed skepticism.

Brian and I squinted across the table at the older woman. Her chic haircut and professional clothing shouted competency. Was it possible this was some sort of scam? After years of believing myself the last of my family line, hearing the woman's unexpected words confused me.

Only the week before, I had despaired of how I could improve my life. Lack of financing limited my options. I had nurtured dreams from my youth about writing the next Great American Novel, but cold, hard reality had worn me down. When your daily focus is scraping together enough funds to pay the rent, high-falutin' ideas about the future go sailing down the river.

"Your uncle, Jack Thompson, passed away. I'm so sorry, Robin." Ms. Miller sipped her coffee, giving me time to process the surprise announcement.

I brushed crumbs from the thin cotton tie-dyed tablecloth, painfully aware of how small and dismal my apartment must seem. Four mismatched chairs surrounded the square wooden table. Rag rugs covered cracked places in the linoleum, but no handmade projects could disguise the outdated appliances or the dripping AC unit, wheezing from the only window in the downstairs room we occupied. I'd rescued the rickety table from the dumpster behind the bar where I worked. A metaphor for my life loomed somewhere in there. I returned my attention to my unexpected visitor.

"Uncle Jack Thompson, you say?" I'd never heard that name in my life. But my mother, God love her soul, had been a flighty butterfly who'd left her restrictive family life behind in her teenage years. Who knew? There might be a whole passel of cousins somewhere, but I'd never know the difference.

My finger traced the handle of my chipped ceramic coffee cup, a souvenir from a rare vacation when I visited the Grand Canyon many years ago. Ms. Miller's announcement had knocked me off kilter. My mother, a devoted hippie in her younger days, had taken the concept of free love to heart and had availed herself of every offer that came her way. Her casual attention to detail ensured I never knew my father. Unfortunately, her carefree lifestyle led to an early grave. No big surprise there. I had expected it and tried to prepare myself to become an orphan from the time I entered high school.

Really, even before she'd died the day after my twenty-fifth birthday, it'd been just me, myself, and I. My gaze flicked to Brian. I wasn't quite ready to count him as part of my family equation.

I studied the well-dressed woman. What was in this for her? Was Ms. Miller's smile artificial, the kind people used when they're in a situation requiring sympathy, but they don't really care? What could possibly prompt her to track me down in San Francisco like this? She mentioned she'd flown in from Texas when she introduced herself.

She gazed directly at me, her look confident and no-nonsense. She seemed the real deal. Her obvious honesty prompted me to resurrect mine. Though the idea of an inheritance tempted, I'd learned the ten commandments. Lying, though near the bottom of the list, was definitely included in the thou shalt nots.

"I'm sorry, Ms. Miller. You've probably come all this way, at great expense, for nothing. I think you've made a mis—"

Brian silenced me with a sharp kick to my ankle. I glared. What the heck? I tucked my feet safely out of reach.

He placed his hand over mine, tugging it from the cooling coffee mug, and squeezed. Hard. His sympathetic demeanor was one hundred percent fake. "Tell us more. We know little about Uncle Jack."

I suppressed the urge to roll my eyes. Brian had obviously skipped the Sunday School lesson about the ninth commandment.

"My involvement began about a month ago. His neighbor requested a welfare check. Several days of mail had piled up, and she noticed an ... well, an odor." She glanced down at the papers in front of her, allowing me to react in as much privacy as possible when seated with two other people in a small kitchen, the scent of last night's curry and rice still flavoring the air.

An odor? Unlikely a scent of Indian cuisine. I struggled to disguise my squeamishness. *Sorry, Uncle Jack, whoever you are —were—but that's just gross.*

"When police entered your uncle's home, they discovered his body in his recliner, TV still on. He appeared to pass peacefully in his sleep." She paused, her look compassionate. "Such a pity when someone dies alone. I'm sorry for your loss."

I almost shrugged. Hard to feel pain for the absence of someone I didn't know. I wasn't fully convinced she was talking to the right person. For the past few decades, my only sense of belonging had come from my relationship with God. Though Mom had never been in competition for Parent of the Year, her passing left me untethered. I was afloat in a sea of dispassionate humanity that swirled past me with as little care as a river rushing around a rock. Acknowledging this new connection would take some getting used to. "And how did you connect me to … Uncle Jack?"

She looked up, brightening. Obviously, she enjoyed this part of her job. "When a person dies with no apparent kin, our office comes in. The medical examiner assigns these cases to me, and I start digging."

"What do you look for?" I couldn't decide if her job was creepy or fascinating.

"I start by searching through files. Correspondence that indicates life insurance or places the decedent may have donated. Often, those papers will designate a beneficiary."

"Robin's name is listed on his life insurance?" Brian failed to hide his financial interest in the pending answer. Heat flared on my cheeks. Ms. Miller would think we were gold diggers.

The woman gave him a measured look. He did not have the grace to squirm. "The only life insurance policy I found was a small one. The funeral expenses used it all." She focused her comments my direction. "When the obvious sources of information fail to turn anything up, I start the detective part of my job. I may find a birthday card still in the envelope it was mailed in, complete with a return address. Or perhaps a photo with a date and names of the people pictured written on the back. I search each name on Facebook, searching for strings that tie things together. Every clue becomes a dot to connect, creating a picture of the person's life."

"He had a photo of me?" I could not conceive of a world where my existence mattered to someone.

"If he did, I didn't find it. But your name was in his contacts file on his phone. It took several days to go through them all, but I eliminated people as possible relatives, one by one, beginning with the As." Modest pride for her perseverance rang in her voice. "I contacted each and interviewed them to see if they were or knew of family members. I spoke with co-workers, bowling teammates, doctors."

"Bowling teammates?" A vision of the creepy bowler in *The Big Lebowski*, lewd sneer on his face, wearing his purple polyester pantsuit, polishing his bowling ball with a chamois towel, flashed through my mind. "My uncle bowled?" Did my scorn for this detail ring in my voice? I dialed it back. Uncle Jack, whoever he was, deserved compassion, not derision. Maybe bowling, like thrifting, had become a retro cool thing to do.

"Indeed, he did. Finally, I came to you, all the way down in the Rs." She cocked her head. "There was no last name, which made identifying you more challenging. I do enjoy solving puzzles." Lifted eyebrows topped her pleased smile.

I frowned, shaking my head. "But why was my information in his phone? I'm positive I've never met the man."

Brian knocked my leg with his knee. He apparently had a plan. And, based on the number of physical assaults I'd received over the past few minutes, my questions didn't match his narrative.

Ill-gotten gains weren't my style.

"They weren't very close." Brian patted my hand.

Scowling, I yanked my fingers clear, scooting my chair away with a jerk. Ms. Miller was clearly more clever than he believed her to be. He would not fool her with this charade.

I wanted to know more about *her*.

"So, you … what? Keep poking around in the lives of dead people until you find someone to inherit their worldly goods?"

Her eyes shone. "Yes. It's quite interesting. Like a mash-up between a professional organizer, an online researcher, and a P.I. Some things I've uncovered over the years might surprise you."

The purple-clad, foul-mouthed bowler and his polished bowling ball flitted through my mind. *Ew.* The private lives of lonely people. I could only imagine.

"What did you learn about Jack?"

She consulted a list on her clipboard.

"He was born in 1950. Enlisted in the Army at eighteen where he served for twelve years. Lived in California for a while."

"Maybe followed my mom?"

"Possibly. He settled in Fort Worth, Texas, in the early 2000s. Never married."

"Texas? I wonder what drew him there." My mother was a dyed-in-the-wool California beach bum. The idea of living in Texas had never crossed my mind. All I knew about Texas I had learned watching *Dallas* reruns on TV and listening to country-western songs. I cradled the warmth of my coffee mug, pondering the heretofore unimagined possibility of family. *God, is this for real?*

Brian fidgeted, clearly uninterested in the draw of Texas. "You, um, mentioned an inheritance?"

The woman shot him a look of barely disguised annoyance. The wattage of her smile dimmed.

"Yes." She answered begrudgingly. "There's an inheritance. Mr. Thompson invested money in a publishing house. Robin, you now own several shares of the Striped

Giraffe Publications. It's a small, but quite respectable, Christian company."

"Really?" My surprise was the first genuine emotion I'd shared with the woman. "How weird. I've dreamed of being published. I have three manuscripts written, but I never felt … well, I doubt they're any good."

She flashed me an encouraging look. "You're an author? This is sounding more and more like it was meant to be."

I lifted my shoulders in a diffident shrug. "I don't know that I can claim the title of author. I've written some stories. Had a few things printed in magazines."

Brian snorted. "She's no Stephen King, that's for sure. What she's good at is serving drinks."

The investigator of dead people blinked. I witnessed the moment Ms. Miller decided to ignore him. She turned a compassionate gaze to mine.

Brian, always the social genius, didn't pick up the signal. "How much is *several shares*?" Avarice gleamed in his eyes. It wasn't a good look on him.

Until today, my sole inheritance had been some bum health issues. I was alone. When I was younger, my doctors had used words like "fragile" and "acute." Things had improved little over the years. Not exactly a popular draw for a swipe right. Brian had provided the only tie to a meaningful relationship, such as it was. Imposter syndrome surfaced in more areas than just writing.

Ms. P.I. shot a thin smile his way, then turned her gaze to her notes. "Your uncle seemed very generous. He donated a kidney a few decades ago. With no obvious living relatives, one can only assume he did that for a friend." She gave me a significant glance. "Possibly a distant family member."

Cold chills prickled on my neck.

"He donated a kidney?" My voice sounded tinny and far away. "When was that? Do you have that information?"

A pleased look crossed her face, and she nodded toward me, giving me the feeling I'd correctly connected a set of dots. A warm sense of accomplishment flooded me, like when I was the first one in Algebra to find the solution to a problem.

"Yes. I tied several of the doctors in his contacts to *that* adventure. He donated on August 13, in 2002."

My breath stalled in my lungs. My finger moved to the smooth, curved scar on my belly, tracing it of its own volition. "While he lived in Texas?" I didn't recognize my own voice.

The woman cocked her head like an inquisitive beagle. "Yes, but he came to California for the surgery." She paused. "Does this mean anything to you?"

I stared at nothing, my gaze turned inward. Did my uncle donate an organ to me? A man I didn't know? Had never met?

"I received a kidney on that date, when I was twenty. They told me only the location of the donor. Fort Worth, Texas. I've always assumed the person died in an accident or something." I focused wondering eyes on her. "Did my uncle save my life?"

"That was my conclusion as well. Your name was only listed as Robin in his phone, but I saw medical records in his file from *his* surgery. A handwritten note was included, apparently from one of the nurses who cared for him at the hospital, assuring him 'Robin' was recovering well, and her body showed no signs of rejecting the donated kidney. I put two and two together, and," she waved her hand toward me, "*voila.* From there, I focused all my attention on you. The crumbs led here."

Unexpected tears flooded my eyes. Why hadn't my mother ever told me about her brother Jack? Why wouldn't she disclose the news that someone in this world loved me enough to share a piece of himself with me? Grief overwhelmed for the loss of all that time. *I had someone. All those years, I had someone.*

Brian did a double take. "You're crying?" An unkind snort of laughter escaped before he remembered to play the part of the grieving almost-nephew. He covered the sound with a cough.

Something welled inside me, rising from the soles of my feet to the top of my brain. Something bright. Strong.

Someone loved me. Enough to store my name in his contacts. Enough to keep tabs on me. To have given me a kidney.

I looked at Brian. "I'd like you to leave." My voice was calm, sure.

He jerked back as if I'd slapped him. "What?"

I'd been loved. My uncle had undergone pain, the risk of surgery, for me. He considered me worthy. The message taught to me over and over in the Sunday School class I'd attended with my best childhood friend finally resonated.

"Please leave. And don't come back."

His face turned ugly. "Robin, you sure you want to dump the only boyfriend who's ever stuck around?"

Blinders lifted from my eyes. My resolve firmed. "Get out."

"The minute you get some money, you're gonna drop me like a used Kleenex?"

I pondered for a moment. Recollections of his unkind words, his selfish expectations, floated through my mind. "Nope. It's not that." The realization that I mattered to someone on this earth—to God—gave me the strength to expect more. To demand better from a life partner.

He exploded from the table, his anger punctuated by the chair tumbling to the floor. He snatched his jacket from the coat rack, muttering vile words as he stormed out.

I walked over and flipped the deadbolt. The sound galvanized me. I turned my gaze to my guest.

Ms. Miller's eyes glowed with quiet pride, and she gave me a quick nod.

"I never knew I had an uncle. And now, I learn he probably saved my life." Things I hadn't felt in a very long time floated to the surface—hope, optimism, confidence.

She returned to her bulleted list. "There's more. He left you his house in Fort Worth, his belongings—he was quite the art collector—and $40,000 in the bank. Plus, those shares in the publishing company, several hundred of them." Her gaze flitted around the small apartment. "From where I stand, you could start your life over again. Follow your dreams."

I could write. Use my imagination to combine words and ideas instead of mixing alcohols to create drinks.

Texas. I could move there. Wide open spaces. Blue skies full of promise and possibilities. God's country.

Tears welled again. I *could* start over. Amazing how knowing you are loved can alter your perspective and give the strength to pivot. I swiped at my eyes. *Thanks, Uncle Jack. And thank you, God, for helping me hang on.*

Greater love has no one than this, that he lay down his life —or his kidney—for his niece.

My uncle healed more than my body's failing kidney. His love healed my life.

Thank you for reading *PIVOT: Stories of Change*. If you enjoyed this anthology, please consider leaving reviews on your favorite book platforms. Your feedback will help other readers discover *PIVOT* and its authors. We greatly appreciate your support!

Scan the QR code below to learn more about the authors and our upcoming books. You can   also visit our website at palmbranchpublishing.com/books.

To stay in the know on upcoming book releases, launch parties, and other book happenings, sign up for our newsletter at the QR code below.

Our world exists in a cosmic sphere of unseen forces.

In this tantalizing compilation of mixed-genre fiction from new and established authors, eleven stand-alone short stories illustrate the mysteries that hide behind the whispers, the sneers, and outright lies. Eleven characters must break through the noise to unearth that which distorts the truth.

Cassie is desperate to convince her father that she has what it takes to be a pilot only to discover family secrets he has been hiding from her. Pato and Boris meet in a shattered post-war future and must decide if they can trust each other in their new climate of technology and survival. Karianne is determined not to fall for her handsome client, all while speculating what the real threat is to his little niece, Ruby. And Lucifer resolves to challenge the Almighty God, demanding retribution for His perceived betrayal.

Just when the fog begins to clear, a new mystery appears.

Journey near and far to discover the **secrets**, the **schemes**, and the **celestial strategies** waiting to be uncovered within the pages of *Intrigue: Stories of Mystery and Transcendence.*

Author Index

Baker, Gary: The Greatest Gift	101
Brucie, Thom: Rising Sublime	195
Jamieson, Erin: Renewal	211
Jordan, Michaele: Vishnu Weeps	43
Lyle, Linda: November or Never	177
Nnoli, Sylvester Chikelue: Beginner's Luck	15
Pal, Sunayna: Teaching Young Kids	147
Pal, Sunayna: The Perfect Cup of Masala Tea	31
Peckham, Paula: A Crazy Little Thing Called Love	225
Rene, Kelley: To Walk In The Park	73
Reyes, Luisa Kay: The Olde Tobacco Bullion Shoppe	115
Rich, Bob: Artist's Revenge	135
Warner, Daniel: The Brother	159
Watkins, Jerry T: The First Girl I (N)ever Kissed	59

For more information, address the licensee/publisher at:
Kelley@PalmBranchPublishing.com
Palm Branch Publishing, LLC
844 N Tyndall Pkwy Unit 257
Panama City, FL 32404
United States of America